Drive Me Sane

DENA ROGERS

CRIMSON
ROMANCE
F+W Media, Inc.

Published by
Crimson Romance
an imprint of F+W Media, Inc.
10151 Carver Road, Suite 200
Blue Ash, OH 45242. U.S.A.
www.crimsonromance.com

ISBN 10: 1-4405-8405-2
ISBN 13: 978-1-4405-8405-3
eISBN 10: 1-4405-8406-0
eISBN 13: 978-1-4405-8406-0

Cover art © iStockphoto.com/GoodOlga

For Dwayne.
Thanks for showing me how amazing the stars can be.

CHAPTER 1

"Who…? Oh, shit!" Sera sputtered, her lips quivering, as she drove up to her uncle's house. She swallowed hard, and her heart slammed into her chest upon recognizing the oversized Silverado pickup truck parked in the driveway. "What the hell is he doing here?"

"I don't know," her friend Maggie answered. "But half the country is talking about that truck."

Sera's quick temper flared. She jumped out of the car, slammed the door, and took a few hasty steps forward, but stopped when her mind caught up with her feet.

He's here.

Looking at the ground, her stomach knotted as full realization of the situation sank in. The man she was once engaged to, who had ended their relationship by voicemail merely weeks prior to her deployment to Afghanistan, was there.

"Tyler!" she screeched, having no clue what she might say when he appeared. Her only thoughts were fueled by almost three years of pent-up anger.

With no movement from the door, her patience thinned. She picked up a piece of gravel from the driveway and hurled it towards the truck. Her unsteady hand missed it entirely. "Tyler Creech!" she screamed again.

Another stone thrown; this time it bounced off the tailgate. She had just grabbed a handful, ready to launch them all at once, when the screen door squeaked open. Pausing, she watched it inch wider until his large form filled its frame. She'd never thought of him as the heartthrob he was portrayed as on country music radio these days. He was a big bear of a guy, full of thick, meaty muscles.

Tall and lean, but never with washboard abs or protruding biceps; however, his body was one to admire.

"Shit," she muttered, meeting his paralyzing stare.

"I see you haven't changed," Tyler stated with little emotion.

Her eyes didn't move as she watched him lean his body into the open door frame. She didn't so much as flinch when Maggie turned the car back down the driveway.

Biting down on the inside of her lip, she tried to think of what to say next. The immediate adrenaline rush was beginning to fade, but it didn't curb her anxiety. Three years had passed since she'd last seen him, and as much as she wished she could say Tyler hadn't crossed her mind, the eagerness of the radio stations to play his newly charted number one hit—and the fact that she'd bought his record—made it difficult. Trying not to let the moment get the best of her again, she swallowed the hard lump that had risen back up in her throat.

"This is my uncle's house, you know." And Tyler's mother's house now too. But Sera left that part out.

He let the screen door swing closed and took the three steps to the porch railing. Leaning over for support, he squinted into the sunlight as he cocked his head to the side and replied, "And that's my truck you just hit."

She tossed a look back over her shoulder. As if she couldn't identify the silly thing. It was every redneck's vision of a perfect ride: big, loud, and loaded with chrome. Maggie was right—it had gained a lot of notoriety after being featured in his music video driving down a muddy road with Tyler serenading a voluptuous blonde sitting next to him.

"What are you doing here?" she asked.

"I had some downtime. I knew Mom and Roy were in Florida so I thought I'd hang out at the house. What are you doing here?"

Sera watched him steadily; his broad arms rested against the wooden railing, his unkempt hair rolled slightly into dark curls at the ends. His full cheeks, despite being bristled with whiskers, had a boyish appearance. *Damn him and his downtime.*

Taking two steps forward she said, "Well, you can't stay here."

"Yeah, well, your uncle is married to my mom now, so I have just as much right to be here as you do."

She closed her eyes, willing the situation away. How much more unfair could life be at the moment? Her ex-fiancé was now her step-cousin. It sounded much worse than it was, but the fact that Tyler's mom was now married to the uncle who had raised her from the time she was sixteen definitely hadn't helped in her quest to forget him either. "Can't you go stay with your dad?"

"Can't you go stay with your mom?"

Grinding her teeth together, trying to keep the bit of composure she'd gained back, she said, "She's two states away, Tyler. I'm not packing up and leaving because you had some downtime." She took a couple of more steps in his direction. Her legs felt weaker with every stride. Yet her stubbornness refused to let her stop.

"Well, I'm sorry to inconvenience your stay. I didn't know anyone would be here."

Likewise, she thought. With a deep breath, she reined in the last bit of her unleashed hostility as she straightened her shoulders and pushed forward, determined not to let the man she'd once loved more than life itself know how badly old wounds had just broken open.

•••

So how long are you in for?" Tyler asked, following Sera into the house and to the kitchen where she stopped for a bottle of water.

She unscrewed the cap, giving him only a quick glimpse of her dark eyes before she tilted it up. He scanned downward, taking in her long hair lying flat against her back before his eyes settled in the heavenly curve just above her hips. Her waist was thinner than he remembered and she looked tired, but other than that, she looked good. Damn good, actually. Clamping down his jaw, he swallowed a gulp of relief, thinking back to the frantic call he'd received from his mom saying Sera had been involved in an accident while deployed. The vehicle she'd been driving was hit by an IED. For days he'd been beside himself, though his mom assured him that no one was terribly injured and that Sera was okay.

Seeing her finally released some of the unease he still carried around, but the awful memory caused a rush of guilt, igniting an urge to get back in his truck and get the hell out of there. He'd imagined this day would come, most days even hoped for it. With his mom and Roy now married, he knew he and Sera couldn't ignore each other for the rest of their lives, but in no way was he prepared for it today. The five-hour drive from Nashville had zapped all his energy, and what he'd thought would be a nice and relaxing visit home was now sure to be anything but.

"I'm here to stay for a while," Sera answered, tipping the bottle up to her mouth again.

So she was out of the army? He wasn't sure how he felt about that—relief in knowing she was safe, disappointed that she hadn't carried on with the only thing she'd ever talked about doing, or angry for more reasons than he could begin to list at the moment.

At the age of sixteen and on the verge of juvenile delinquency, Sera Cavins had come into his life after being sent to live with her uncle. Roy's sole priority had been for his niece to graduate, and although Sera quickly settled in and flourished in their minutely populated town of Cobb City, Kentucky, college was never something she'd given much thought to. Instead she'd enlisted in the army a week after graduation and shipped off for basic training two months later. "So I guess you had enough of military life?"

"Yep," she answered, swinging around on her heels toward the hallway.

"When did you get out?" he asked, following her to the doorway of her room. She paused long enough to give him a short glimpse of the chestnut color in her eyes, eyes laced with all the hurt and anger of the past few years. He winced at the thought before hearing her say that she'd been back in town for a week. Then, without giving him a chance to say anything further, she quickly closed the door.

CHAPTER 2

After lying restless in bed for more than two hours and hearing Tyler strum idly on his guitar, never putting more than a couple of chords together at a time, Sera gave into the insomnia that plagued her most nights and got out of bed.

His music had always reflected his moods and his inability to work through a song echoed his failure at forming clear thoughts, letting her know that whatever was on his mind was as heavy as his obsessive pull on the strings of his guitar.

Wondering if his unsettled mood was solely about her presence, or if something else was bothering him, she walked down the hall knowing good and well she should leave him alone. Contact with Tyler was the last thing she needed. She'd hoped to take the time alone while Roy and Diana were in Florida to try and find her way back to being the Sera that they all knew, or at least some semblance of the woman they remembered. She missed the vibrant person she once was, but didn't know how to find her again. It seemed life was drifting by just outside of her reach. She wanted to grab on and go with it, yet the weight of the last few years kept holding her back.

Nearing the end of the hallway, she considered turning back around. Earlier in the day she'd promised to keep distance between them. But following rules, even those she'd set out for herself, had never been her strong point, and instead of going back to bed like she knew she should, she found herself standing in the entrance of the living room, gnawing nervously at her lip while admiring a barefoot and shirtless Tyler sitting on the edge of the couch.

There had never been any frills that came along with knowing him. You got what you saw and from what little she had kept up with his career, it seemed something he'd stayed true to even in his rise to celebrity. It was something she greatly admired, although at times she wanted nothing more than to hate him.

It was still hard to watch his video and not think of the silly guy she used to date. The one who dressed up in drag one year for Halloween, the guy who toilet-papered the principal's car as a prank their senior year, the guy who could make her laugh at the drop of a dime, who picked her up and brought her home nearly every day from school, whom she had spent almost every waking hour with. The man with a voice that could make grown men cry.

He was also the one who, on the brink of her deployment overseas three years into her service, decided his career was more important than having a girlfriend fighting a war.

With the bitterness from earlier in the day giving way to the curiosity of knowing how his life had been, when all was quiet, she said, "I'm sorry about your truck."

• • •

Tyler looked up at the sound of the voice that had been echoing through his head for the last two hours. He could still picture her out in the yard, chucking rocks, horribly annoyed with the idea of him being there. Her temper had always run high; her feistiness was just one of the things that had attracted him to her all those years ago. Raised in inner-city Chicago, where life wasn't nearly as laid back, she wasn't anything like the mild-mannered girls he'd grown up with and he'd quickly found that he liked the company of someone who always pushed. Who never gave in just to save face. It was her softer side that had driven him wildly in love with her, though. A troubled childhood had brought out one of the most compassionate people he'd ever met, but it had also fed her insecurities and vulnerabilities, making her a hard one to understand at times.

Seeing that her mood had lightened, his lips curled up and he shrugged his shoulders. "Hey, it's just a $60,000 truck."

Sera moved to the couch, dropping down on the opposite end and folding her knees up under her. "Why do you need a $60,000 truck?"

"I don't," Tyler answered. "But I didn't pay for it."

"Of course you didn't," she said, mirroring his sarcasm. "I suppose part of becoming a rock star means you have a vast amount of vehicles at your disposal."

He really didn't like the presumption Sera was making. Of all people, she knew how hard he'd worked to get where he was at and it hadn't stopped. He still busted ass every day to keep his career moving because he didn't want to go down as a one-hit wonder like so many other artists did.

"It's not my truck, Sera. I get to use it as a promotion. You know, I drive a new souped-up Silverado to promote my song that talks about driving a jacked-up truck. In exchange I mention the dealership that loaned it to me. I recommend them on occasion and they get to use my name in their ads—come buy your truck where Tyler Creech got his. That sort of thing." He gave her a wink as if she should know how the music business went.

"So you sold out?"

"No. I like the truck. I like the owner of the dealership. We both get something out of the arrangement."

She folded her arms over her chest. "Well, again, I'm sorry."

Setting down his guitar, he settled into the corner of the couch. Gentleness had come out of the bedroom and he hoped to take the opportunity before her fury returned to request some civility between them, although he knew he deserved none. All the wrath that had come pouring out of her in their first few minutes of seeing each other was warranted. In fact, he'd always expected worse.

"Sera," he began, then stopped when he glanced over and saw a strand of hair hanging down around her curious face. Resisting the urge to reach out and smooth it back behind her ear, he ran a frustrated palm overtop his own hair, annoyed with his inability to talk to the woman he'd once planned to marry.

Even after three years there were days he still couldn't believe they were no longer together. He'd thought the twelve months she was deployed was difficult, but the two years since her return to the States hadn't been much easier. He might have ended it, but it had never been his honest intention. Stressed with his career taking off and her imminent deployment, he'd lost his temper—which was so unlike him—and said things he didn't mean. Instead of apologizing like he should of, he'd let it go when Sera had nothing to say in response. Why? He didn't know, except that Sera always had something to say and when she didn't, he was lost as to what to do.

He missed her like crazy, thought about her more than he knew he should. He hoped her life was going well, but he also didn't want to know any specific details either. Especially if she'd been able to move on, because he hadn't been able to. Thankfully, his mom seemed to understand that, because they rarely spoke about Sera. The only two things she'd ever told him were about the accident and that she'd arrived safely back home.

"Damn, this is awkward," he said, unable to ask for the forgiveness he so desperately wanted.

"Yes, it is," Sera finally let out with a dry laugh. "So, aside from it being weird, you want to tell me what's on your mind?"

There it was. Her sweet, gentle side that was still so damn easy to love. She'd always known his moods and was never afraid to call him out when he was stuck in one like he was now. What was on his mind? Did she mean besides her?

"Trying to figure out what song should be released next."

"It's just a song, Tyler. It's simple. Pick one."

"Actually it's the follow up to a hit, meaning it's going to be held to a higher standard."

"I'm sure no matter which one you pick, it's going to do great."

"I hope so," Tyler answered with a heavy feeling inside. He didn't quite have the same confidence. His track record had proven fifty-fifty. The first single he'd released had fallen flat. He was lucky his label had moved forward with the second, hoping that it did better. Apparently there was a hillbilly trend in country music and they liked hearing him sing about riding around in a big truck with a pretty girl by his side. He quickly wondered if Sera had heard any of the songs on the record, or more importantly if she knew he'd written every one of them. If the next song failed, he feared he may drop down on the promotion list and lose a lot of the backing he had. Unfortunately in the music business, it didn't always matter if you could sing or not. Sometimes it came down to who was pushing to get your music out on the radio. "So what's got you up so late?" he asked, hoping to change the subject.

"Couldn't sleep." She stood, giving him one last look as she said, "Go with your gut," and turned back toward her room.

He watched her disappear back down the hall, admiring the hint of flesh that showed through the thin, white, calf-length cotton gown she wore. She dressed more like a woman his mother's age rather than the stunning twenty-five-year-old she was, yet somehow she made it sexy.

When he heard her door close, he flung himself back against the couch and thought about what she had said about his gut. He knew it was in reference to his music and what song he was thinking about, but his gut was telling him it was time to make things right with her.

CHAPTER 3

Sera looked at the clock. Almost one. Half the day was gone already. She wondered what time it had been when Tyler finally went to sleep the night before. For a long time after their short talk, she'd lain awake hearing him play the same tune over and over. Each time, she tried to put a name to the notes that sounded familiar, but nothing ever came to mind. The last time she looked it was almost three o'clock, but she honestly had no idea when she'd actually drifted off.

She had purposely staying camped out in her room this morning, hoping to avoid as much contact with Tyler as possible. But realizing she couldn't stow away all day, she finally emerged, ate some toast, and showered before going outside to inspect his truck.

Bending down, she rubbed her hand over a nickel-sized dent and cringed with shame at how quickly she'd lost her temper the day before. More than that, she hated that Tyler had seen the unpleasant act. Of course, at the time, none of that had mattered. All that mattered was the one person she absolutely didn't want to run into was exactly the one who'd shown up.

"Looks like we got a vandal running around."

Startled, Sera jumped back, covering her hand over her chest. Her heart took off like a jackhammer, the irregular beats making her unsteady. Blowing out a few small puffs of air to rein in her pulse, she looked up to find Tyler standing a few feet away. His hair stuck up in all directions with a long piece swaying across his forehead. His long basketball shorts and a University of Kentucky T-shirt were the total opposite from the worn jeans from the day before. "Jesus, you scared me," she said.

"You all right?" he asked.

With a nod of her head, she said, "Yeah."

Straightening her shoulders, her eyes instinctively looked down as the fabric of his shirt stretched across the width of his chest when he crossed his arms behind his head. Then, realizing what she'd done, she pulled her face back up to meet his. Cupping her hand over her forehead to shield the sunlight, she tried not to obsess about how good he still looked or let his closeness get the best of her again.

"I thought you'd given up your delinquent ways." Tyler gave a look down towards the spot where she'd seen the small dent.

Sera glanced away. Her short fuse had actually tamed the past few years. Extra duty and more pushups than she ever wanted to admit had cured her bad habit of speaking her mind and lashing out. Overall, she couldn't deny her time spent in the army had been a good experience and the structure she needed; but it had also come with a price that she was still paying even though her time serving had come to an end. Unfortunately, the sight of Tyler had brought back the ugly side of her personality she'd thought had ended as well.

She knew he was joking by the way he kept smiling, but as the pace of her pulse rose and her palms moistened, she also knew she was on the verge of losing control again too. She could feel warmth rising out of her chest, although she wasn't sure if it should be blamed on the heat from the bright rays bearing down or the way Tyler's eyes fixated on her. How could he appear after almost three years and act as if all was all right? Every time she looked at him, she felt like a raving lunatic, with an array of emotions running wild. She wanted to scream and yell, then break down and cry for all the heartache he'd caused.

Tyler was the one constant in her life. Or had been, anyway. The one person besides Roy whom she'd been able to count on for anything and everything. The one who knew her better than she sometimes knew herself, who pushed her to be a better person. He had no idea how difficult her deployment had been, knowing she didn't have him to come home to, and now after three years, he stood right in front of her, acting as if no time had passed.

Knowing that if she stood there much longer some sort of talk would ensue—and likely even more harsh feelings spew, or maybe even tears—she bit back the snappy reply she had lined up. "Like I said before, I'm sorry about the truck."

She walked past him, back into the house.

•••

Full of guilt, Tyler lay on the couch, more listening to the television than watching. In the six hours since Sera had disappeared back to her room, he'd more than once been tempted to pack up and head back to Nashville. Leaving now, though, would end any possibility of making the past right, which he'd already decided he wanted to do. But how to go about doing that was the problem. He couldn't read Sera as well as he used to. Provoking her, as he'd done earlier in the day, used to break down her defenses. It hadn't worked in his favor this time, and he wasn't really sure how to reach out when she seemed so far away and different. There had been a time when he'd known everything there was to know about her. He could calculate her mood just by the way she walked. Now, though, when she spoke, she was reserved and cautious. He hated knowing that they had come to a point where they were no longer comfortable with one another.

The sound of her door opening jerked him up into a sitting position, but then he lay back quietly pretending to watch TV again when she walked through the living room into the kitchen and began looking through the cabinets. He considered offering to take her out to eat, thinking it might help ease some of the tension between them if they could sit down in a neutral place and actually have a full conversation, but then decided distance was probably best since she hadn't so far shown any interest in being in a room with him for more than a few minutes at a time.

Besides, the view gave him the opportunity to admire what he'd only been able to see in the picture that he still carried around in his wallet. Her hair, a milky shade of brown, swung loosely around in a long ponytail as she moved around the room. He used to love to run his fingers through the soft strands and remembered how soothing Sera said it was for her as well. When she bent over to get a pan out of the lower cabinet, he couldn't help but think just how perfectly his hands had wrapped around her slender hips. Pleasuring each other had always come naturally. Sera could work magic on his body, just as he knew exactly what turned her on. Then again, everything between them had come easily and simply, except for those few months before she deployed to Afghanistan. There had been nothing easy about that time.

• • •

"Are you hungry?" Sera yelled from the kitchen just as she heard Tyler's phone start ringing.

"Yeah," he answered back, before saying hello and taking the call out to the porch.

After spending the entire afternoon in her bedroom thinking about the situation, she'd decided she couldn't take the constant strain. Tyler was there. For how long she didn't know, but she couldn't stay in her room for the next couple of days, much less weeks if that was the case. Besides, if she ever wanted to move forward in her life, she had to let go of the hostility she still held onto. After all, moving on was the reason she'd come back to Cobb City.

However, letting go proved harder than she'd imagined when the two of them sat across from each other at the table. She fidgeted with her napkin, trying to make small talk about her Uncle Roy and Tyler's mom, Diana, but that ran dry and awkwardness took over, sinking them back into an annoying silence. In between bites, she stared off at the bland white walls, wondering how it was possible that she didn't know what to say to someone that she'd once shared so much with. It was just a matter of time before the past crept up and an inevitable talk ensued. Their relationship hadn't ended on a clear note; however, for now she was content to put it off for as long as possible. If she was lucky, maybe Tyler would soon be on his way and then they could get back to forgetting about each other all over again.

When they were done, Tyler seemed all too happy to get away when she dismissed his offer to help clean up the kitchen. Not that she minded. The taciturnity had her ready to escape back to her room. But then she heard a long strum of his guitar from out on the porch and stood at the sink, unable to move. The next few notes had her setting the plate she'd just rinsed aside and leaning against the counter to listen more closely. His fingers danced with the strings. She closed her eyes, getting lost in his music. She loved to hear him play just as much as she enjoyed his voice.

Unsure of how long she stood there, she opened her eyes when she started humming along. She didn't allow herself to play his album that often, but she'd listened enough to recognize most of the songs. But hearing them with a full band and Tyler singing the lyrics was completely different than hearing only the guitar's acoustic version as she was now.

Drying her hands, she stood still, slipping back to the soulful sounds. With each new song, she grew more curious about his career, until she was caught up in the excitement and momentarily forgot all about the strain between them. She was at the door, ready to go out and listen for a while, when she heard the familiar tune from the night before start up again. The chords were slow and saddening. Closing her eyes, she searched for the words she knew were there. They came just as Tyler finished strumming the chorus. *She got a trip around the world and I got a box of regrets.* She'd love to hate that song. She didn't have to ask to know it was about their breakup. The lyrics too closely resembled details of their life together. And although she could recognize its beauty, it was also heart wrenching to hear at the same time.

"Track number seven," she stated, pushing the door open a little with her foot.

She recognized the surprise on his face and couldn't hold back the smile that came with knowing she could still read him so easily. "I like 'Blue Jean Kinda Night,' too," she said shyly.

"Someone bought my record." Tyler beamed, his mood completely different than the solemn way he sat through dinner.

"Did you really think I wouldn't?"

"Honestly?" He shook his head with a throaty chuckle. "No. Not unless it was to smash it into a million pieces."

"Such faith in me," she joked, seeing for the first time a small resemblance of the man she used to know. "So track seven seems to have you hung up. Is that what you're considering next?" Anxiety over the answer filled her stomach.

Tyler hesitated. "I'm just not sure about it."

Sera thought on that for a moment, and decided that it was a subject better left untouched. She offered a straight face. "Again, I'm sure whatever song you choose, it will do just fine." Then, moving her foot, she let the door close and went back inside.

• • •

Tyler set his guitar against the railing and leaned back into the swing, wondering if Sera would ever sit still long enough to have a decent conversation with him and if she did, would he figure out what exactly to say. Every opportunity he had to try and talk to her seemed to sneak up without warning. Like the night before when he wanted to apologize and instead coughed out how weird it was that they were both there. Their time at the dinner table came and went without one thought leaving his mouth and his chance just now seemed only like it might be an opening for an argument. She'd obviously heard the song yet refused to call it by name, which didn't leave him all that confident about how she might feel if it was released. He'd written "Box of Regrets" while trying to cope with the guilt of losing her. He'd broken her heart once. He wasn't sure he could consciously live with himself if he broke it every time she turned on the radio.

CHAPTER 4

Staring at his reflection in the mirror, Tyler saw lines extending out of the corners of his eyes that he hadn't noticed before. He wondered what the women who hung around to flirt after his shows might think if they could see him now. The rugged appearance he wore on stage took more to attain than most realized. If it were as simple as pulling on a pair of jeans and a T-shirt and going out to sing, life would be easy. But it wasn't. In fact it was stressful and tiresome and sometimes he wondered why he wanted to do it in the first place. The circles underneath his eyes were evidence of that. They were usually masked by all the lighting on stage, but in Roy's well-lit bathroom they boldly stood out. Life on the road was taking its toll on him—and not in a good way.

With half of another day already wasted by his continuing the never-ending chase for a good night's sleep, he hopped in the shower, hoping to summon up some motivation to take advantage of the rest of the day. The hot water felt good against his tense shoulders, but it did little for the slight throb in his head. Then again, it seemed he always had a headache lately. The constant stress of being on the road and all the added attention from his hit "Endless Night" didn't help. Interviews, charity events, fan meet-and-greets. You name it, he had been there. It was to the point he couldn't even rely on a day to rest while on the bus in route to his next show because he was too busy catching late-night and red-eye flights just to keep up. He hadn't stopped for the past four months; hadn't spent more than three consecutive days at his own house in Nashville. And while he'd considered staying there while off, he knew his mom and Roy were in Florida, and he believed being surrounded by the simple things from a time when music had been a way to pass the time and not so much work would help him make peace with the release. At least that had been the idea, until he found Sera there. How ironic it was, that he was now sharing a house with the reason he was in the dilemma to begin with.

He half hated that he'd chosen to put the song on the record. Of course, everyone had fallen in love with it. It was an emotional love song. A wonderful ballad. At least two top-notch artists had asked to record it, to which he'd declined. He'd written the song, poured his soul into it, and he had no interest in letting someone else try to convey the feelings it possessed. But damned if he was ready to throw all that out to the world to hear.

The absence of footsteps tracking across the wooden floor and lack of whisper from the TV had Tyler scouting the house for Sera when he came out of the bathroom.

A look in the living room and kitchen showed no signs of her. Her bedroom door had been ajar when he passed so he knew she wasn't hiding in there again either. A bit of worry and irritation came when he stepped outside and didn't find her on the porch or in the yard.

Fearing maybe she'd left without saying goodbye, he went back to her room and saw her nightgown strewn over the end of the bed. Personal items still littered the dresser. It didn't appear she'd left for good, but then he couldn't count anything out when it came to the things she did. He'd never imagined she'd walk away from their relationship without something to say, but she had.

Needing a break from the place that was a constant reminder of the only woman he ever loved, he got in his truck and headed to town. He made it a little over a mile down the road when he saw her walking. A laugh fell out of his mouth. Again it seemed that fate had stepped in and placed the very thing he was running from right in his path.

Slowing about thirty feet away, he enjoyed the gentle twist of her hips and swinging of her arms in perfect rhythm as her feet tapped lightly against the gravel road. It wasn't until he stopped completely that she turned around, showing a face full of trepidation. What he'd do to know what was going through her mind. Did she really hate him? She had every right to. Or was she both happy and sad to see him at the same time? More importantly, did she still love him? In any possible way? She had no reason to, but he couldn't help but hope that what they'd shared had been too special, too meaningful just to evaporate into air. At least, it had been that way for him.

He rolled down his window. "Going somewhere?"

•••

Sera inhaled a deep breath through her nose and held it for a moment. If Tyler didn't stop sneaking up and scaring the shit out of her, she was liable to make a complete fool of herself. Crossing her arms over her chest, she glanced down. She needed some space. She couldn't go through the day holed up in the house with him again and she'd go stir crazy if she tried to stay in her room any longer. Every time she looked at him she felt a pull. Longing for the familiarity that they shared tugged her one way, while her broken heart pushed her the other. She tried to be angry because that at least felt good for a few seconds, but then as soon as it disappeared she remembered all the good times they'd had.

She was a mess. Heck, she was a mess without Tyler there. Add him into the equation and she felt like a blooming freak show. "I needed to go into town."

"Did you consider driving? It's five miles there and back."

No, she thought. Actually it had never crossed her mind. She'd sold her old car after getting back from Afghanistan. With most things on base within walking distance she saw no need to rush out and buy another and since she'd only been back in Cobb City a week, she hadn't even considered it yet. "I don't have a car," she answered.

"All you had to do was ask. You're welcome to mine anytime."

She eyed the large vehicle in front of her. That definitely wasn't happening. Giving him a prudent face, she said, "Oh, I can imagine myself driving this bus. No, thanks!"

With a goofy grin and a tilt of his head, he said, "All right then, hop in. The bus will at least give you a lift."

Her shoulders sagged as she walked around the front of the truck and opened the door. Hoisting herself up at least two feet off the ground, she sank down in the bulky leather seat and buckled her seatbelt. She really hated his truck, or rather the vision of the blonde in the video riding in the exact place she was now sitting. The woman smiled flirtingly over at Tyler, her full red lips licking each other as if she were a sex kitten ready to pounce. Sera had no idea who the actress was, but was certain she hated her too.

"So where are we headed?" he asked, forcing her to look up at the gravel road ahead.

"The bank, grocery store, and post office, but you can just drop me off at the bank. I can manage from there. Maggie will bring me home when she gets off work."

• • •

Stopping in front of the post office, Tyler saw the slip of annoyance Sera gave him as she got out of the truck. She wasn't happy about his refusal to simply leave her at the bank like she asked. However, he saw no point in making Maggie run her around when he was plenty capable of doing it. She didn't appear as irritated when he drove to the grocery store, and even waited for him to catch up when he got out and followed her in. Tagging behind, he watched her shop with a curious eye. Trash bags, toothpaste, bread, and cheese; she dumped them all into the little red basket she carried around after reading each of their labels. Tyler didn't spend much time in grocery stores—he was never in one place long enough to need much—so this task was actually pretty fun. He was especially entertained watching a lady in the produce aisle feeling up a head of lettuce. When the lady walked away, he gave Sera a wave of his eyebrow. Her cheeks rolled into dimpled balls, but she held back the laughter trying to escape.

"Was she feeling for lumps?" he whispered, when they stopped by the apples. "I swear she fingered the stuff like a man touching a woman's breast."

A small chuckle broke free, turning her cheeks a cute shade of pink. She covered her mouth, wrangling it in, but it was too late. Hearing her first genuine laugh since their reunion somehow stitched up a wound inside he didn't know he had. He couldn't pass up the opportunity to rile her up some more and hear it again when they passed the cantaloupe. Picking up two he held them to his chest and grinned at her excitedly.

"Put those down," she spat. "You're embarrassing, you know."

"Yeah, I know. You've told me a million times."

He loved to tease her. She was the outgoing, always-ready-to-say-what-was-on-her-mind,   it-didn't–matter-who–was-around type—but he never failed to bring a smile to her face.

They were in the truck on their way to the bank when he started wracking his brain for a way to extend their time together. Some of the tension was beginning to fade and for a few moments in the grocery store it had been much like old times, with the two of them cutting up and having fun. But as soon as they pulled to a stop, Sera thanked him for the ride, said she'd see him later, and got out. Frustrated that once more she'd bailed as soon as it seemed they were forming some kind of truce, he sat thinking about how much she'd changed. Aside from her rock throwing, she wasn't anything like the spunky woman he remembered and he wasn't sure he'd ever get around to having the talk that they should have had three years ago if something didn't give.

Sitting in the spot where she'd left him, he rolled down the window when the bank door opened and Sera walked back out. "Hey. Everything all right?" he yelled.

"Yeah, Maggie won't be off for almost an hour. She's going to meet me at Merv's."

Feeling as if he'd finally caught a break, he threw back, "That's where I was headed."

CHAPTER 5

Situated in the foothills of the Appalachian Mountains, Cobb City lacked almost everything except charm. Not that it was desolate. It had all the things a small town needed. There was even a five-man police force that patrolled the streets, as well as a few small businesses that came and went over the years. There were also a few places that had come and planted roots. The Dairy Freeze was a favorite spot far past the county line and Riley's Auto Parts didn't seem to have a problem staying afloat. Neither did Merv's.

"Well, look who the cat drug in," Merv drew, as Tyler and Sera walked through the tiny hometown bar's door. "Sera, I heard you were back in town, but Ty—man, I haven't seen you in ages."

Merv shook Tyler's hand before turning to Sera and gathering her between his burly arms for a hug. The overgrown beard and belly reminded her of a redneck Santa, minus the white hair and red suit. He was a jolly sort of fellow too, happy and ready to help anyone that came in.

"So what brings you two back? I thought you'd both moved on to bigger and better places."

"Just here for a visit," Tyler said.

Sera looked around, hoping the conversation passed right over her reasons for being home. She didn't want to explain her early departure or the circumstances that led to her involuntary discharge from the army. It was still a situation she was struggling to accept herself.

"Get a seat, stay a while," Merv said.

Tyler took a chair at the closest table; following behind, she sat on the opposite side, letting Merv claim an empty seat between them when he brought back three Cokes.

Just as quickly as they sat down, they began reminiscing about old times, and any awkwardness vanished when Sera began throwing out her own memories of the place.

She and Tyler had started hanging out at Merv's when Tyler became serious about his music career at the age of seventeen and he talked Merv into letting him play a set one Saturday night. That one set became an every weekend event until Tyler realized that if his dreams were going to go anywhere, he needed to branch out and start playing gigs elsewhere. Soon he was traveling to surrounding towns, playing larger bars, making his way to the bigger cities and nightclubs, before heading to Nashville. Sera had never doubted he would make it big. She'd just assumed she'd be along for the ride when it happened.

When Maggie showed up a little after four, she brought a couple of girls from the bank with her. They all sat crowded at the tiny table, talking about old times. Eventually others gathered and before long, half the bar was listening to Tyler talk about his buoyant life on the road. When Maggie stood, saying she needed to get home, Sera looked at the clock and saw it was almost ten. She hadn't realized they'd been there that long, and aside from one overly flirtatious girl who'd made eyes at Tyler the whole night, she'd had a good time. She noticed that even Tyler had smiled, laughed, and appeared more relaxed than she'd seen him the previous two days. It hit her then how much she'd missed his goofy smirk and how she still thrived from seeing him happy. Unfortunately the thought also made her wonder how many other women Tyler had charmed with his humble ways. Had there been anyone special that enjoyed looking at him as much as she did? Aside from listening to his music, she tried really hard not to think about the life he lived. A life that they were supposed to share. But it was hard to turn a blind eye to all those thoughts with him there. A dull ache formed in her belly as a vision of the blonde from his video flashed through her mind. For all she knew Tyler could have had many women.

"You ready?" he asked, as Maggie left the table.

"Yeah." She swallowed, grabbing her purse.

The envy only worsened when they were back in his truck and she got her first good, long look at him. During the stolen glimpses of the last few days, she hadn't been able to see past the ex-boyfriend part to be able to really appreciate everything he was. His raw features were eye catching. The stark contrast of his dark eyes against his pallid skin made it difficult not to want to dive into their depths. She'd gone there once. She knew how good it could be, but fear of what might happen if she went there again had her head ringing with warnings.

Lost in those thoughts, she didn't realize Tyler had stopped the truck until it was too late. She hadn't heard him announce the train was coming or tell her to get out so that they could stand by the side of the tracks to feel the rush of it passing—something they'd done countless times as teenagers. It wasn't until her door opened and he was there tugging on her arm that any of it began to register.

The blow of the train whistle entered her body when she opened her mouth to beg him to leave. It stole her voice and threatened to suffocate her lungs as it traveled down her throat, then settled somewhere deep in her chest. The tightness was unbearable, as was the buzzing that vibrated every vein running through her limbs.

"Come on, Sera."

He pulled on her hand and she quickly snapped it away. The pounding of the rails as the train flew by ricocheted through her head, drumming up a harsh pounding.

"Sera," Tyler called again.

No, no, no! she thought with a shake of her head. Her hands covered her face when the images flashed. Dizziness came as she started holding her breath. She closed her eyes, willing the demon away even as she told herself to breathe. *Breathe, dammit!* She couldn't. The night sky faded into a miserably bright sunny day and suddenly she was back to a place she didn't want to go. Then came the sound—*whoooo whoooo*—just before the loudest, most unpleasant horrid noise blasted all around.

"Sera. Sera," Tyler yelled, shaking her wildly.

Her whole body shuddered. She cried out, "Oh God," when an image of Rollins's bloodstained face popped into her head.

"Sera. Dammit! What's wrong?" Tyler screamed.

She shook her head from side to side, swallowing hard, letting the flow of air trickle down her throat. With her lungs full, the images began to fade, as did the inherent pounding of her chest.

"Sera," Tyler yelled louder.

She opened her eyes, barely able to see through the tears flooding her face. Tyler's hands were on both sides of her shoulders, shaking her roughly.

"Sera, dammit, talk to me."

She opened her mouth, but only sobs came out. Her hands and feet trembled as wretchedly as her heart had been a few seconds before. She breathed heavily, trying to catch her breath, but another cry stole it. Finally, she looked up. Tyler's eyes, thick with fear, bore back at her.

"Are you okay?" he asked.

Closing her eyes again, she couldn't bear to look at him. No. No, she was not okay. She gave a nod of her head, saying she was anyhow.

"What the hell just happened?" he barked.

Another whimper escaped as she continued to wrangle in the uneven breaths. Then, looking away, she said, "Please take me home."

CHAPTER 6

The sound of the bedroom door opening had Sera quickly trying to muffle her sobs. She wiped at her face, trying to dry any lingering tears. Why she thought her fast bolt from the truck would save her from an explanation, she didn't know. But then she hadn't worried about a talk. All she wanted was to get away from the hollowed-out look Tyler kept giving her. As if he wasn't sure if he should be concerned for her safety or his.

How crazy he must think she was, if something as ordinary as a passing train sent her into a fit. It had all happened so fast. She didn't have time to prepare for her reaction and so she freaked out instead. Now on top of feeling the emotional toll the episode had taken, she was embarrassed too. A silly train. She couldn't even watch or listen to the whistle of a silly damn train without losing it.

Another swipe of her face ensured that the flow had stopped, but she was thankful for the near darkness that hid what was surely her reddened face.

Feeling a give in the mattress, she looked up to see Tyler sitting on the opposite side of the bed, facing the wall with his elbows resting against his knees. His head bent down and his shoulders slumped forward. He looked as battered as she felt.

His voice sliced like a knife through the black silence, pushing all tension and anger aside, leaving only a genuine concern between them. "How bad is it?"

He knew. He knew without having to ask. But then of course he would. He was a smart enough man to figure it out. As much as she wanted to tell him to screw off, she couldn't. This was Tyler. Not some nosy busybody interested in her life for no good reason. She recognized his sincerity as what it was: a true concern for her well-being. Quickly thinking about her answer, she searched for a blasé excuse to hand him, but expelled the truth when she opened her mouth. "Not nearly as bad as some."

. . .

Tyler felt like a piece of him ripped away, as if nothing he thought true was right. Sera had come back from Afghanistan physically unwounded, but she was suffering in a way neither he nor could anyone else really understand. She hadn't been acting quite right, but he hadn't been able to put his finger on it and chalked her weird behavior up to seeing him. He was sure his presence wasn't helping matters, but she was dealing with more than just the awkwardness of meeting up with an old flame. She had PTSD, post-traumatic stress disorder. He'd only imagined possible physical wounds, nothing else, because Sera had one of the most strong-willed minds he'd ever met. "Is that why you got out?"

Hoarsely, she answered, "Yes."

"Was it voluntarily?"

"No."

The fact that they were having this conversation was bad enough, but hearing the aridity in her voice and knowing Sera wasn't the type to let anything get her down, stabbed his already tormented spirit. Running his hand through his hair, he fought the urge to grab her and hold her against him. He couldn't stop thinking about how her mouth—a mouth that was normally so full and pretty—had twisted into a ring of awful terror. Nor could he forget the way her shoulders and arms had shaken as violently as the rails of the train tracks. He'd almost been afraid she might fold over into her sobs and fall out of the truck. He'd even imagined her body withering to the ground and wondered if he hadn't been there to keep her in place what she might have done. The sound of her cries continued to echo in his ears.

Never in his life had he wanted to hold her so badly, yet the sheer look of being entirely somewhere else halted the need. He thought he'd heard Sera at her lowest before her deployment, when she'd called every other day on the verge of tears while lashing out. But that had been about him and her concerns for their relationship. It had nothing to do with a fear of carrying out what she'd enlisted to do.

Knowing he'd been quiet for far too long, he stretched out beside her flat on his back. She lay motionless with the covers pulled up high to her neck. He knew she'd lie like that all night without another word if he didn't press for more. Yet he had no clue of what to say either. Finally gaining some ground on the flood of emotions filling his body, he asked, "Have you talked to anyone about it?"

"I have. It didn't really help."

"There's medication they can give you."

"I know all about the crazy pills."

He wasn't sure if her obvious offense to the medication annoyed him or filled him with relief to know she hadn't changed as much as he thought. After dabbling with drugs in her early teen years before coming to live with Roy, she'd sworn off even drinking. It was one of the many things they had in common, because having an alcoholic father made him leery of the stuff as well.

At least now he knew that it wasn't him keeping her up at night. Although he wished it was. He could put his guitar away and let her sleep. She couldn't tell the nightmares or whatever else haunted her dreams to give her peace.

Not knowing what to say next, he turned over, facing her rigid body, and hated what his soft, lovable Sera had become: a hard, broken, and distant woman. The need to reach out and touch her became almost consuming, but he knew it wasn't the time to act on selfish impulses. Balling his hands into fists so he wouldn't do just that, he asked, "You want to talk about it?"

"Not really," she said, and paused before speaking again. "I don't want your pity, Tyler. I don't need it. There are a lot more that come back with far more difficulties than what I'm dealing with. So please don't look at me or treat me like I'm fragile or crazy. I'm not going to shoot up the town or go berserk. I know that's what people think when they hear PTSD. It's not like that."

He almost laughed. Just when he thought the woman he used to know had all but disappeared, her spunky side came through. "You were crazy before you went into the army, so I don't associate the two together." Joking, he threw her a smile he knew she couldn't see. However, when she turned toward him, even in the darkness, he sensed she wore one as well. "Talk to me, Sera."

After a few moments she finally said, "It wasn't all that bad. Mostly my time went fairly smoothly. Being away from all your friends and family is the worst part."

A pain seared through his torso. She'd been lonely. Of course she had. Thousands of miles from home in a country full of people who didn't want her there and the one person who'd promised to love her for the rest of her life had walked out merely weeks before she'd gone. It wasn't exactly what he wanted to discuss. He hoped for more of a direct explanation of what happened, but as long as she talked, that was all that mattered. His conscience would just have to suffer through and deal with the guilt of his past actions later. "Did your mom not write?"

"She wrote. And your mom and Roy made sure I received something every week. I got so much stuff I had to start giving it away."

More than once in those twelve months he'd thought about writing her. He had even typed out a couple of emails, but he could never bring himself to hit send. Her lack of response to the ending of their relationship had told him more than any words could. She was hurt beyond words and the thought of reaching out, only to be ignored again, would have been harder to bear than hearing her lash out. Thinking she just needed some time, he thought she would come around eventually, if for nothing more than to give him a piece of her mind. That hadn't happened either. Not once since she returned from Afghanistan had she tried to contact him, nor had she acknowledged the tickets he'd sent her to his show in Austin shortly thereafter. He'd taken the chance of them both being in Texas to try to reach out. He didn't know if she went and couldn't blame her if she didn't, but it was the last hope he had to try to get back the girl who had literally knocked him off his feet. A small laugh escaped with the memory of her first day of school in Cobb City.

"What?" she asked, clearly seeing he thought something was funny.

"I was thinking about your first day of school here."

Not one bit happy about coming to live with her kidless uncle, whose wife had died and lived in the middle of nowhere, Sera was a hellcat on wheels. Her first month there was nothing but battle after battle. Roy had rules to follow and chores he expected her to do, which weren't things she handled very well since structure had never been a part of her life. Roy also didn't let her get by with much, not even when her sharp temper flared and she pushed Tyler after he bumped into her while playing volleyball in the gym. There was no major squabble. Caught off guard, he stumbled backwards to the floor. They stared at each other sternly until she walked away, but when he got home that afternoon, Roy brought her over to apologize. Apparently one of the other kids had gone home and told their parents all about the new unruly girl at their small town school, who in turn took it upon themselves to call and let Roy know just what a handful he had taken on. Sera later told Tyler that having to apologize to his mother for acting like a five-year-old was the first time she could remember being truly embarrassed about something she'd done. She also said how surprised she'd been when he was waiting at her locker the next morning. From then on, they were practically inseparable.

"I was a little high strung," she said.

"You think?" he teased again.

"Come on, seriously. I wasn't that bad."

No, she wasn't, he thought. In fact, she was pretty damn cute, the reason he'd purposely bumped into her, trying to get her attention. He got it all right, and then she got his and she'd had it ever since.

"Nah. Actually you're quite adorable when you're mad."

When a long silence followed, Tyler wasn't sure what he said, but it was clear he'd said something wrong. Sera breathed in deeply and then he heard a faint sniffle.

"Sera, what's wrong?" With no response, he rubbed his thumb across her cheek to ensure he was correct. The moisture immediately tightened his chest as did the turn of her face away. "I'm sorry," he added.

"Sorry for what?" Her voice broke as she continued to fight the tears.

Sorry for being an asshole. For letting you go. Allowing you to go through all of this on your own. Not being there when you needed me. "I'm sorry for hurting you." That pretty much summed it up.

"Don't," she said with a shake of her head.

Her last word came out fragile, radiating the ache in Tyler's upper body to his arms all the way down to his stomach. More tears followed, cutting his injured soul open further.

Unable to thwart temptation any longer, he reached out, prepared to meet her resistance when he pulled her close. But instead of fighting him, she settled into the crook of his shoulder.

CHAPTER 7

Before Sera had the chance to pry her eyelids apart, her heart rate fluttered toward the ceiling. The irregular beats rushed the flow of blood through her veins so fast that she was sure her eardrums would explode. The unbearable throbbing kept her pinned to the bed, unable to move. Nightmares weren't usually her problem. Once asleep, she normally stayed there. It was the drifting-off part that she had trouble with.

Trying to remember what had been so terrible as to wake her in the middle of the night, she blew out a few small breaths, gulping back the saliva stranded in her throat. It wasn't Rollins's blood-soaked face that popped in her head. Tyler's tormented eyes were what she'd been dreaming about.

With her pulse slowing, she finally opened her eyes, but it wasn't dark, like she expected. A slice of daylight cast through the window, showing off the mid-morning sun. The sharp rays reminded her of the lights from the train from the night before. It wasn't a dream. Tyler was—turning to the side, she saw Tyler lying next to her. The incident by the railroad tracks was real. A flush of embarrassment came as she recalled all the details. The train, her meltdown, her and Tyler's talk, her crying, then the two of them laughing and then her crying again before the sleeping pill she'd taken right before she slipped into bed took effect. The last thing she remembered was not having the energy to fight the strength in his arms as he gathered her into him.

She hated to cry more than anything and now she'd done it not once, but twice in one night. The tears she'd shed for Rollins were easily explainable. It was a traumatic experience even if no one lost their life. However, the tears that came when Tyler began flirting weren't as easy to acknowledge. He said she was adorable when she was mad, which may not have been much, but she knew Tyler. She knew what that low drawl in his voice meant, and it hurt so badly to know that he could forget how callous he'd been. After planning a future together, he'd ended their engagement with a few words left on a voicemail.

Trying to derail the downturn of emotions that were again piling up, she glanced at the clock and saw it was after nine. A decent night's sleep in comparison to the couple of hours that she normally got. Yet the rest didn't resolve her fatigue. Every one of her muscles ached like they did every other morning, and her eyes swelled from the tears she'd shed. If only she could get through a day without feeling like a tightly wound-up jack-in-the-box, ready to pop at any given moment. Everyone kept saying in time it would get better, and some aspects of her disorder had, but others seemed stagnant.

Lack of sleep and the inability to do certain things still interrupted her quality of life, as the army psychiatrist put it. *Quality of life—ha!* She didn't really care how great the quality of it was. She just wanted it to be her own and not dictated by something that had happened to her.

Ready to forge some distance, she sat up, happy that she and Tyler had fallen apart at some point during the night. At least she didn't have to add "waking up tangled together" to her list of regrets that morning. But as she took one long look at his thick shoulders before leaving the room, she couldn't help but think how good it felt when he touched her. Even with all the hurt of the past, she still found comfort from being in his arms.

• • •

Tyler paused just inside the kitchen. Sera sat at the table with one leg pulled up in the chair and wrapped tightly with her arm. Her head cocked slightly to the side, throwing her long hair over a shoulder as she pored over a crossword puzzle book. She would have looked peacefully engrossed if it weren't for the constant tapping of her pencil against the tabletop. The intrusive sound conveyed clear agitation on her part, which left him somewhat relieved that she was already out of bed when he woke. He'd had two pretty shitty days so far, and he hoped to bypass another if at all possible, and waking up together would have definitely jump-started another toxic day.

After pouring a cup of coffee, he sat at the table, trying to work up the courage to bring up the night before. A week ago, the only real problem in his life was that of his upcoming single. Now he stood under a waterfall. The problems kept piling up and pouring over top of him. All of which revolved around one thing, or rather person: Sera. How was she going to feel about the release? And how was he supposed to find some contentment when the two of them were barely speaking while staying under the same roof? Which brought upon his biggest problem of all: making things right between them was no longer enough. From the moment he saw her standing out in the yard, he knew all the feelings he'd been trying to ignore were still there. He loved her. Simple as that. All the proof he needed was the feeling of completeness he had while she'd slept in his arms.

Any progress they might have made was gone, though, when she didn't so much as look up to wish him good morning. He should have expected as much. She was never one for easily confiding her feelings. It had taken more than a year after moving to Cobb City before she began telling him about her life in Chicago. A life so different from the small-town upbringing he'd had. He couldn't begin to imagine the disjuncture of having to attend a different school each year because her mom found a newer or cheaper apartment in another part of the city. The absence of a father or even a name of the man who'd helped create her had never helped either. Not to mention the string of boyfriends Sylvia had in and out of the house. Some were kind to Sera, while others preferred she wasn't around. By the age of ten she was staying at home by herself while her mom worked the night shift. By thirteen, she was sneaking out at all hours. It wasn't until the police brought her home stoned for the third time that Sylvia decided she needed help. Roy stepped in. Tyler didn't want to think about where Sera's life may have led if he hadn't. Yet she'd never let any of that beat her. She was tough, that was for sure, but even the tough needed someone to lean on from time to time.

After turning his coffee cup around in circles for the better part of five minutes, the silence began to wear on him. "Sleep well?" he asked.

•••

"Yeah," Sera answered, swallowing down just how well she'd slept with him there.

Somehow in the span of the ten minutes since Tyler walked into the kitchen, she'd forgotten that she was supposed to be keeping distance. The hour-long talk she'd just had with herself about how she couldn't get swept up with how good he looked or the familiarity of their past and the fact that she still somehow trusted him was as if it never happened. All she could think about was how good his arms had felt around her in those few minutes before she drifted off to sleep.

"Have any plans for the day?"

Detecting a strain in Tyler's voice, as if he was trying his hardest to keep the flow of words coming steadily, but with apprehension at the same time, she forced her head down. She didn't want to look up and see what she knew was there. Tiptoeing around what he wanted to say infuriated her. She hated when people treated her differently because of her problems. Yet she also knew it could work to her advantage too. If things continued to be awkward between them, they'd be less likely to have canoodling little chats like they'd done the night before.

"No," she replied back, keeping her focus on the paper in front of her. She wasn't even sure what number on the puzzle she was working on. Her thoughts were stalled on him and his close proximity. She was pretty sure his eyes were glued to her, but she didn't dare look up to see. She reread one of the clues, but then realized she'd already answered that number and went to the next. Looking over it once, twice, three times and still unable to comprehend a word she read, she jumped ahead to the next.

"Flag," Tyler announced.

Confused, her head popped up. Tyler leaned in much too close, his face turned down at the crossword. A whiff of his scent drilled inside her nostrils.

"Flag," he said again, moving his hand to point at a number on the page.

A brush of his finger across her arm had her jerking back in response.

"Old Glory," he said, attempting to clarify. "The answer is flag."

Flag, she thought looking down. Her brain, however, wouldn't relay the message to her fingers. His hand continued to invade her space, just as his eyes still raided her privacy. She wasn't sure if she wanted to claw them out or rip off his shirt. Her emotions were suddenly so off kilter. Tossing the pencil, she pushed the paper aside and leaned back in her chair, staring at him much like she did that first day. "Quit looking at me like that."

"Like what?"

The control in his voice riled her even more than the smug grin and crinkle at the corner of his eyes. He knew exactly what he was doing—driving her crazy, crazier than she already was. "I don't know. Like…" Like, she didn't know what exactly anymore. She wasn't even sure why she was angry again.

"Like what, Sera?"

At first she thought it was pity. His eyes did crease in a sympathetic way, but the sexy turn of his lips looked awfully lustful. Oh, hell! Maybe it was just her subconscious wanting him to lust after her, like she was doing him. Feeling the spiraling, she stood, needing some space before she let it all out. "I prefer if you just didn't look at me at all."

She made it to the door before Tyler jumped up, thrusting his hand against the frame to block her exit. "Going to be hard being in the same house and not looking at each other for the next two and a half weeks, sweetheart."

Two and a half more weeks? She'd barely made it through the last two days. And sweetheart! Where did he get off calling her sweetheart? Her legs weakening, she begged him with her eyes to let her through. Refusing to physically push her way past, her stubbornness wouldn't let her vocally ask, nor would she demand; because that would only result in Tyler demanding something in return—most likely a talk. She couldn't handle a talk right now. Not yet. Finally, as if he too saw the fight falling away, he stepped aside and dropped his arm.

• • •

Once more, Sera was nowhere to be found when Tyler came out of the shower. He'd given her a pass in the kitchen. He'd had her right where he wanted, on the verge of letting it all go, and then he'd stepped away. He couldn't do it. He couldn't be a bastard and force something he knew she wasn't ready for. Not with everything else she was going through.

More than two hours later the screen door swung open, startling him from a nap. Her only explanation of where she'd gone came by way of an expressionless look before she went to the kitchen. She didn't so much as glance his way when she went back outside. Frustrations building, he jumped off the couch and looked out the window. He expected a reinforcement of some of her defenses, but he didn't deserve the silent treatment.

Moving to the door, he watched her fill the push mower with gas. Glancing over at the riding mower parked in the shed, he shook his head. "Where did you go?" he asked bitterly, thinking back to her words from earlier. She didn't want him to look at her. How she could even conceive the idea was crazy. He did nothing but want to look. She was beautiful in the most natural way, the kind of woman who never needed an ounce of makeup to impose her beauty. It was also a completely unfair request since she'd been looking at him too. She might be trying to hide it, but he saw and she could pretend all she wanted. They still had something between them.

Descending the steps, he saw her gaze dart up and then back to the gas can as she twisted the cap back on the jug. "To town for gas."

Growing more agitated with each passing second, he asked again, "Is there a reason you didn't ask me to take you?" *Besides the obvious—she hated him again.*

Sera let out a huff. "Tyler, look … I don't want to fight with you, but I don't know what you expect me to say either. Let's just let this go and try to be cordial the next couple of weeks?"

The mower roared to life as she pulled the string and then took off, padding across the grass. He let her take about ten steps before bounding out after her.

She cut the engine and planted her hands on her hips. "What?"

"Why aren't you using the riding mower?"

She glanced toward the shed then back at him, her face creased with discomfort. The weight of all her thoughts piled up inside her head. He wanted them to pour out. To hear what she had on her mind, to give him some sighting of the woman he used to know.

"I don't know. I just thought I'd use the push mower," she answered.

Feeling like he was losing the battle, he cursed under his breath. Then, mimicking her actions, he drew his hands up to his hips. "Why are you doing this?"

"Doing what?" she practically yelled.

"Fighting this?"

"Fighting what, Tyler?"

Each of their voices grew louder with every word. Tyler pressed his lips firmly together, annoyed with his lack of restraint. This talk, like the one he planned earlier, wasn't going anything like he hoped. But for whatever reason, he couldn't seem to stop himself either. "You're fighting me."

He regretted it the moment it left his mouth. Her pulse raced through the vein in her neck, forcing her chest to thump heavily with each breath she took. Why was it at times he could talk to her senseless and then others like now, he knew nothing to say?

"Fighting you? Is that what you think I'm fighting?"

The piercing sound of her voice reverberated across the lawn. She closed the space between them like a bee buzzing to pollinate its next flower. Except Sera's face didn't resemble any flowering beauty, and there definitely wouldn't be any pollination, although he would have gladly accepted the offer if she were agreeable.

He stepped back in apprehension of a push from her hands, but the only force that came was the finger waving erratically in front of him.

"You?" She thumped him in the chest. "Has life become all about you? You, Tyler, have no idea what I'm fighting, and trust me, it has nothing to do with you."

They'd been here before. He and Sera had often fought, mostly about inconsequential things that amounted to nothing and usually it was because he was pushing her to say or admit something she didn't want to. But even with that knowledge, he knew when to stop. And everything within him said he needed to stop right now. But he couldn't.

"There's still something here, and you're fighting that."

He expected a snide comeback by the snarl of her lips; however, when she continued to stare at him as if she couldn't believe what he'd said, he went on. "You think the last three years have been easy on me? You think I wanted what happened? We were supposed to be married by now. Maybe starting a family." He shook his head. "I don't understand why you thought I might cheat on you. I never did anything to make you think I would."

"Shut up," she spat, taking a step back.

The look of horror on her face smacked him. "I never thought …" He swallowed down the guilt. "I never thought you would let me go so easily."

This time her lips quivered. He flinched in reaction, but didn't stall the step he took in her direction. He wanted to cover her mouth and smother the pain away for both of them, but he stopped when Sera stepped backwards in unison. Unable to match her unnerving stare, he looked off to the side. "It was never supposed to be like this."

"And what exactly was it supposed to be like?" she asked.

The sudden strength in her voice forced his attention back to her face, but before he could expel the truth, she went on.

"Did you think you could waltz back in and that we'd take right back up where we left off? Because now things are easier for you? Because you've arrived and aren't struggling anymore? I'm sorry to disappoint you, but that's not the way it works."

Clamping his jaw tight, he let the rush of guilt again settle over him as Sera turned back to the lawnmower. The thunder of the engine gave clear indication that the conversation was over. Trying to think of something to say, not wanting this to be the end, he stood still for a few moments.

Closing his eyes, he thought back to that awful day when the life he'd always pictured slipped away. Sera had called just as they were loading the bus in the piss-pouring rain, ready to leave for a two-week run of small-town bars. It was the cruelest type of shows: late nights in little named towns with a rowdy bunch that couldn't care less about the free music being played. A small flat fee was paid, but Tyler made little to nothing from the gig himself.

He'd dashed back to the awning of the gas station, already soaked, to take her call, and much like all the other recent conversations they'd had, she grew anxious within a few minutes of saying hello. Her words came out short and sharp. Everything had been a battle for them for the last several weeks. He tried to calm her down, but nothing worked. He knew she was worried, but she had no idea the turmoil and stress she put him through each time they spoke. More than a thousand miles apart, her in Texas ready to deploy and him in Nashville on his way north, there wasn't anything he could do to ease her mind other than listen. That proved to be more and more difficult with every call.

The constant accusation of him finding someone else while she was gone pissed him off. Sera knew him, knew he wasn't that kind of man, yet she continually threw it out. It was like she was trying to break him down. Had been for weeks, and on that raining day, he teetered closely on the edge. He wasn't sure how they were going to get through the next twelve months without both of them going completely insane if something didn't change. Just as the bus driver yelled his name, indicating it was time to go, she threw out the allegation again. That was when he finally broke.

Sera, I can't do this anymore. I can't keep on like this. I've got too much going on right now. Those three sentences said so much, yet they didn't. He wasn't even sure what they meant when they came out of his mouth and it didn't help that she didn't say anything in return. *Tyler!* the driver yelled again. He put a finger up to say he'd be a minute longer. *This isn't fair to either one of us.* Another long silence came and then the line went dead. He wasn't so surprised as much as mad that she'd hung up on him; she'd done it before. Angry, he crammed the phone back in his jeans, ran across the water-soaked parking lot, climbed on board, and settled in for a six-hour drive to some small town in southern Ohio. She didn't answer when he tried to call back three hours later. If there had been any confusion about what he meant, the voicemail he left cleared it all up. *I think this is for the best. Maybe we both need a break. Be careful. I love you.*

Unsure of how long he'd stood watching Sera make trips across the yard, he gave her one more look, then went back inside to the guest room, pulled out the plastic bottle from inside his suitcase, and popped a small orange-colored pill into his mouth.

CHAPTER 8

Knees bouncing, Tyler darted his gaze from the clock on the wall to the door and back. When seven o'clock came and went, he gave Sera until eight to come home. At eight, he decided to wait until nine before he went looking for her. It was a quarter till.

She'd taken off again just as soon as the pill he'd taken did its job and knocked him out for the rest of the afternoon. It was after five when he woke, and without a word from her, crazy ideas hung in his head. Where she might be or whom with. Maggie? Maybe, but he didn't have her number and wasn't sure if she still lived in the same place. He thought about driving out to check, but really didn't think he'd find Sera there anyway. They were never the kind of close friends that shared deep feelings. Actually, Maggie had probably shared a lot. It was Sera who didn't divulge often. This could only mean she was likely off on her own, traipsing around in the dark—God, he hoped not, but with her, anything was possible. She'd once hitchhiked home, from one of his shows in the next town over, because they'd had a disagreement. He'd been out of his mind that night, but even more so now.

Their argument that afternoon left him greatly concerned. He'd pushed her, and then kept doing so, trying to make her say something—anything. And then he didn't like her response when she did. She made it sound like his love was contingent with the timing of his life and whether or not it was going smoothly. His career was taking off and he was already burning out, while she was suffering in a way he couldn't begin to understand. It definitely wasn't the ideal circumstances to try to win your old girlfriend back, if you asked him.

Unable to sit still any longer, he jumped up and headed for the kitchen. Running his hands under the faucet, he patted his face and just turned around to check the time again when the phone rang. Instead of calming, it only pricked his already wild nerves.

"Hey, Ty, it's Merv. Hate to bother you, buddy, but I think you should come down here."

Whatever the reason for Merv's call, Tyler knew it had to do with Sera. The crazy images materialized again. Had she picked a fight with another patron? Gone on a drinking binge and acted out? The latter was less likely but a lot of time had passed. A lot had changed. Not taking the time to ask, he hung up, saying he'd be right there.

· · ·

For a Wednesday night, Merv packed in the house. Only a few tables sat empty as Tyler scanned the room, ignoring the music ringing in the background. No familiar faces popped out at him, but then he was only concerned with one in particular.

Not finding Sera at any of the tables, he surveyed the bar and saw Merv standing in the doorway next to the rear entrance. Slowly he made his way there, unsure if he was ready to see what he may encounter. The idea of her belligerently drunk and outside puking was the only conceivable theory and it tore at his soul to think she'd sunk that low.

"Hey," Merv said when he was near.

"Hey," Tyler offered back, giving a fast look outside the door, once more disappointed that he didn't find Sera.

"I didn't know who else to call," Merv explained.

Tyler searched the back parking lot in the direction Merv pointed. He saw Sera sitting in the grass about ten yards away from the railroad tracks with her legs pulled up and wrapped tightly with her arms against her body. She looked lost, completely lost.

"How long has she been there?"

"She came in about four thirty this afternoon. Sat at the bar for about an hour or so, then got up and walked out the back door. When she didn't come back in, I went looking for her and found her out there. She told me to go to hell. She's been sitting there ever since. It was getting late, so I figure she needed to get home."

A bit of fear crept up with worry that Sera's condition might be worse off than he'd imagined. He hated considering the option, but had no other viable reason for what she was doing. "How much did she have to drink?"

"Just a Coke. We talked a bit. She seemed completely sober to me. A little sad, maybe, but I figured the two of you might have gotten into a spat or something."

With that, Tyler made his way out the door and across the lot. He reached the grass just as the signal sounded for a coming train.

"Shit." Timing definitely wasn't on his side today.

His first reaction was to run to and herd her away so as not to have a repeat of the night before, but his curiosity to understand what she was doing overruled the idea to shield her. She'd been out there for hours. A train passed roughly every three. She'd endured the tragedy at least once on her own.

As the signal grew louder, she covered her ears. When the whistle blew, right before the train approached the crossing, she started rocking back and forth. The air in his chest thickened as he saw her body sink into a shudder as the first car passed. Even from where he stood the pressure of the train cutting through the night could be felt. The evening air pushed back, and Sera sat practically underneath, taking it all full force, hearing the cruel sounds without any kind of buffer.

With the last of the cars out of sight, she slumped forward, resting her head on her knees. A large lump formed in his throat, and the stinging rise of bile coated his neck. Swallowing hard, hoping to make it disappear, he began making his way to where she sat, but each step exemplified his unease. The tightness that had started in his stomach was everywhere now. His lungs felt as if they were about to combust. His shoulders constricted with every step he took and his head blazed with a troubled fury as the understanding of what she was doing came. It wasn't any kind of suicide attempt. She was there to torture herself.

The rigidity dissolved a little once he was seated next to her, but then only enough to allow him to breathe. Unsure of where to start, he was once more lost for words for the woman he still desperately loved. He damned himself for being clueless on what to say or do when she needed him most.

They sat for what seemed like ages until finally Sera broke the silence.

"Merv call you?"

She'd regained some control. Tyler hadn't looked at her directly to know she'd been crying. He saw the way her body convulsed though, and heard the sniffles that were trying to replace the sobs that were there just a few moments ago.

"He did." There wasn't any point in lying. She'd be able to see right through him.

Another silence dragged on. Tyler picked at a blade of grass, attempting to get a handle on his emotions. "Why are you doing this?"

• • •

Sera looked straight ahead. Why? The answer was so simple, but she was sure Tyler wouldn't get it.

"You think I'm crazy, don't you?"

"Are you trying to make me think you are?"

"No."

"No, Sera, I don't think you're crazy. Having a hard time with something, yes, but not crazy. In fact, if you sat in the house all day being pleasant and nice, then I might question it. You were never the kind who sat back and let something take you over, but I don't understand. Not this. Why would you put yourself through this?"

Sera thought about what she wanted to say. She had so much bundled up inside. There was so much Tyler didn't know. No one knew. PTSD had so many different layers and degrees to it that it was a hard condition to figure out. Not one affected person acted or responded the same and while some knew what triggered their episodes, others weren't so lucky. She wanted to count her blessings. Trains were an obvious prompt for her breakdowns and while she had once tried to avoid them, she was tired of running from her problems. Running wasn't helping. Whether she eluded any sightings of them or not, the memories were still there. Somehow she still found her way back to that day beside the tracks in Afghanistan. The sad part was, the thought of a train had actually brought her comforting memories in the moments before the blast. But now all it was was a reminder of what had happened.

At times, the guilt was so incredibly unbearable she thought it might do her in. Not that she would ever consider the option. It was the physical weariness that wore on her. The mental exhaustion that kept her in fits. Every day, she got up feeling as if she were battling something—except she wasn't sure what it was. She wondered if stress could really kill a person, if she'd just go to bed one night and not wake up. The idea was fearsome. Likely the reason she didn't want to fall asleep.

It wasn't the way she wanted to live. She didn't want the rest of her life stalked with bad memories and sleepless nights. She wanted some normalcy again. To do the things she always dreamt about. The things Tyler had mentioned earlier that day: get married, have a family. A job wasn't anything she'd really ever considered because her future had always revolved around Tyler's career, but right now, she'd take that over wallowing in her own self-pity.

She hadn't given any of that much thought since returning from Afghanistan. Her focus had been on dealing with her disorder while trying to stay in the army, but when she couldn't do that, she'd come back home, hoping to heal. But instead of rebuilding her life, the pain had been cut deeper when she had to face Tyler, the man she once believed she'd share all those dreams with.

Her rollercoaster of emotions had done a loop after their spat that afternoon. He'd flipped her world upside down once again by merely saying that he hadn't wanted what happened between them. Well, if not, then why had he done it? She wanted so badly to ask, yet she was afraid to know the answer. Along with everything else, she was confused about why she'd kept badgering Tyler about cheating on her. It was never a genuine concern. She had just been so darn angry at the time that she seemed to pick a fight every chance she got. It was a lot to swallow now that she thought back on it.

Despite all the uncertainty, she knew she was losing the battle to stay angry with him. She hated how he still had the ability to take her from fighting mad to calm and vice versa on a flip of a dime, which was what the past few days had been like. One minute she was ready to uproar and the next they were cuddling in bed like the lovers they once were. She was afraid to go there, especially now that he had laid the groundwork for some kind of peace talk, because if she'd found herself in bed with Tyler on ugly terms, she could definitely see herself there if things were friendlier.

Which would only give him the power to break her heart all over again, and that was something she couldn't deal with. Not now. Not with all the other madness going on in her life. Wanton dreams or not, Tyler wasn't the man to fulfill them for her.

Remembering that he'd asked a question that she hadn't answered, she conveyed the gist of what she'd just considered.

"I just want to be normal again. I don't want to live like this, Tyler. I want more out of life and if it takes me sitting here every day until I can do so without awful memories going through my head, then I will."

"Sera, there are other ways. You're torturing yourself."

"I've tried other ways. Nothing helped. I did one-on-one sessions and group therapy. I hate doping myself up just to get through a day. I don't know what else to do other than face the problem head on."

She sensed some understanding when Tyler draped an arm over her shoulder and pulled her into him. It went completely against everything she had just told herself, but she rested against his shoulder and let him hold her anyway.

It wasn't until she closed her eyes again that she felt him brush a kiss to the side of her face and say, "I'm proud of you for being so brave."

A tear slipped down her cheek. He'd be deeply disappointed if he knew she wasn't nearly as brave as he believed.

CHAPTER 9

The smell of coffee filtered down the hallway as Sera made her way to the kitchen. It wasn't her usual drink of choice; she much preferred a glass of juice or water in the morning, but the aroma was enticing. After pouring a cup, she looked out the window, seeing Tyler's long body slumped down in the porch swing with his legs stretched out over the banister.

Even though it was after ten, she was surprised he was awake. Since arriving, he usually slept in much later than that. She couldn't blame him with the hours he kept. He'd been awake when she fell asleep while listening to him thumb his guitar. She'd fought the urge to get up and listen more closely, or try to talk about the problems riddling him. His song release was apparently more of an issue than she'd imagined. She'd figured that out when she noticed every time his music was mentioned, his face crinkled with strain. It wasn't the effect she remembered it having on him and she hated that something he loved so much was bringing him distress.

He'd given her another pass. There was no prodding or pushing when they left the tracks. He'd taken what she said and left it there. She appreciated his kindness, especially after what she'd put him through the last two days.

His presence had really thrown her off, but after thinking about it more, she imagined the situation couldn't be any easier for him. They'd loved each other. Not the kind of love that passed through your teenage years and you never thought about again, but the kind you build a life around and promised forever. Sharing a house with someone with whom you'd broken those promises wasn't easy. Both of them were also running high on emotions from their individual problems too, which only made the situation more complex. The smart thing would be for one of them to leave, yet neither had. That had to say something, other than the fact that she loathed the idea of going to Chicago and knew Tyler would be completely insane if he spent one night at his father's. He could have gone back to Nashville, which seemed like the more sensible idea, but he was content to stay, even with all the strain between them. She couldn't imagine why.

She'd thought about that while sitting out by the tracks yesterday. She thought a lot—something she tried not to do that often. But while her usual obsession fueled the guilt she carried, yesterday's unearthing was more about the person she was, and who she wanted to be. She'd been pretty selfish in the past. Not with material things or her time, but emotionally. Her feelings were her own, not anyone else's, and she didn't do well when others hammered at the walls she built. Tyler had always been the exception to that, or so she'd thought. Along with a lot of other things yesterday, she realized she'd held back from him too, and that the ending of their engagement was just as much her fault as it was his. So, if their relationship wasn't as strong as either believed, then what was he doing there now, when it would be so much easier if he left? *Trying to make past sins right—sins he didn't entirely commit.*

• • •

Hearing the start of the mower, Sera put down the book she was reading and went to the window. Tyler had abandoned the swing. She scanned the yard, seeing the push mower where she'd left it, then went to the back door to see what he was doing.

He was making his way across what was more of a field than a lawn on the riding mower. She watched for a few moments, her eyes following along the straight lines he drove, the grass piling up neatly behind. She tried to concentrate when she went back to her book, but the picture of his lean body kept pulling her away. After twenty minutes of staring at the same page, she got back up and went to the door again. The August heat, even before noon, was intimidating. On her third trip back, he'd shed his shirt. The thick muscles were marred by an uneven farmer's tan. She giggled quietly. Celebrities were supposed to keep up with their appearances, but apparently Tyler hadn't gotten the memo. Weirdly, though, she was attracted to the pasty skin on his chest. The area called to her, saying *touch me, touch me.* She imagined doing so, running her palms along the widths, settling them in the curve of his waist. Tingling, she looked away, hoping to distract the warm kindling down below. There had been no tainted thoughts the night he'd crawled into her bed. She'd been too upset to acknowledge anything other than that she still found him attractive. However with her mood more amiable and him half naked, she longed for more than looking at him. She'd been with only one other person since Tyler, and as much as she cared for Rollins, they'd never had the kind of chemistry she and Tyler had.

Sitting down on the back steps, her head moved back and forth with every trip Tyler made across the lawn. She didn't even try to hide the fact that she was looking at him. He knew she was there. He flashed a big grin and she waved back. It was silly that the simple gesture made her all giddy inside, but it did.

By the time he pulled up and stopped in front of her, the tingling had her squeezing her thighs together. She felt like a hormonal teenager, because only a teenager could find beads of moisture rolling down one's neck erotic. She bit down on her lip, combating the urge to lick the wetness away. He reeked of a mixture of earth and salty sweat, but somehow she even found that enticing.

"Need something?" he asked as he turned the mower off.

Grateful for the distraction, she asked, "Do you want something to drink?"

"Water," he answered, swiping his arm across his forehead.

Okay, so she was definitely in a hormonal tangle—and pretty sure her lips could do a better job of absorbing the dampness than his forearm had.

She stood, uneasy from the flames sparking through her hips. "Sure." She nodded. "I'll be right back."

Grabbing a bottle from the refrigerator, she let it swing closed with a little more force than she meant. What was wrong with her? Staring and excited over seeing Tyler naked. She'd seen him naked plenty of times—fully naked, at that. His lack of clothing wasn't the only reason she couldn't get him out of her mind. She'd been thinking about him since lying in bed last night. Their talk at the train tracks had somehow brought her some resolve and despite her reservations of becoming involved with Tyler again, in those moments before she drifted off to sleep, she really wished for the comfort of having him there with her.

• • •

After coming in from the yard, Tyler noticed a missed call from his manager. He went to the porch with the intention to return it, but then went back inside without doing so. Seeing that Sera was making dinner, he took a shower. He gave his phone another look as he pulled on a pair of jeans. After pulling a T-shirt over his head, he dialed. Almost immediately, he was greeted with the false air of bullshit that he'd become accustomed to when it came to dealing with Bradley.

"Hey, Tyler. My man. How's Kentucky?"

"It's good," Tyler answered, already knowing what the call was about.

"So we've got a deadline. What do you say? Can I give them the go ahead for the song?"

A pull in Tyler's shoulder tightened. It was just a song. Wasn't that what Sera had said? "I'm still not sold on it."

"Ty, look. The label is breathing down my neck on this. They wanted it announced weeks ago and agreed to give you a few days. They want it out there before this tour kicks off, which is a little more than two weeks away. There's a lot that goes into promotion. You know that. It needs to be on the air by the time those bus tires start rolling."

"Yeah, I know." Tyler rubbed the back of his neck. Some of the tension he'd woken up with had eased during the day, but as soon as he heard Bradley's voice it was back.

"So give the okay on the damn song. Quit making this difficult. You're going to shit this away if you don't."

"I gave them other options."

"And they were clear that this was the song they want next. They want to show your softer side. You've done the hyped-up redneck thing. Let's let the fans know Tyler Creech isn't just a beer-guzzling, chick-chasing Neanderthal. That he's had heartache just like everyone else."

Bradley had no idea how true that statement was. He didn't drink, nor actively chase women, and he'd seen more than his share of heartache, which was the problem. The song wasn't something that came to him sporadically in the middle of the night. He wasn't feeding off a friend's despair. He'd bared his soul in that song and he wasn't sure how the other person involved might feel about her life being heard by millions.

"Give me till tomorrow."

Bradley sighed. "Tyler, you know they're going to do what they want anyway. They're just trying to make you feel as if you have a say and to let you think you're included."

He was well aware of that. It was in his contract. Something he definitely intended to address when it was time for renewal. "One more day," he reiterated.

• • •

Sera knew something was off when Tyler sat down to the table for dinner. Gone were the silly grins he'd been using to try to hide his tired and ragged face. In their place were lines of worry extending around the edges of his lips, and a deep crinkle in his forehead that illustrated his thoughts. Was there more going on that she didn't know about? Or was he worked up solely about the next song?

It didn't take Einstein to know his dilemma. He'd casually mentioned that he wasn't sure how it would be received and she had good inclination that he was referring to what she thought of it. Two days ago she would have sworn that he was guiding a knife slowly into her heart and turning it ever so lightly so she could feel every inch of its blade. But some resolve had come to her yesterday. With the decision to more or less fight for her life back or the life she wanted, she also came to the conclusion that it was time to let go of all the animosity with Tyler. Like she'd already admitted, she knew she had a good hand in his decision to end their relationship, and it was time that she let bygones be bygones.

With little talk at the table, she began missing the easiness of the day. They'd sat on the back porch and talked for more than an hour when she brought him the water. Mostly catching up about Roy and Diana. It was a safe topic, one she appreciated after the polluted thoughts that came from watching him mow. It was also a nice way to spend the afternoon. However, the evening had turned cumbersome again.

After helping clean up, Tyler returned to the porch. Sera had left him to his thoughts that morning. But with the compassion he'd shown the last couple of days, she couldn't continually ignore that he was stressed out too.

Standing in the doorway, she looked out into the darkness. Uncle Roy lived down in a little holler, as the folks around there called it. It was a small gully carved in the hills where the sky darkened quicker than in town and the surrounding wilderness overpowered everything around, making the space feel like a box once night fell. Even after living in Cobb City for almost nine years and thinking of it as home, she still couldn't say the word like everyone else. *Haller*, she pronounced to herself, unable to attain the accent that Eastern Kentucky folks had. *Hollow*, she said again. The word never seemed to run properly off her tongue.

"Only eight o'clock and it's dark already," she said, stepping through the open door.

• • •

Tyler turned with Sera's voice. He didn't need her to remind him that they had run out of daylight. Soon the darkness would also disappear, announcing another day had arrived, which meant two things. One, he had a call to make, and two, he was one more day closer to leaving. Three weeks had sounded like forever upon his arrival, but it was passing by too quickly. There was too much to do, too much to say, and way too much to make up for in too little of time. "Just think, in a couple of months it'll be getting dark at like six," he replied.

"Guess you'll be living the high life again by then," she said, smiling at him.

God, how he missed that smile. She was beginning to do it often too. Not that he was complaining. He enjoyed seeing the pleasure radiating out of her. "The high life isn't all it's cracked up to be."

Glad she'd come out, he took a seat in the swing, and then patted the spot next to him for her to sit as well.

"Really?" she asked.

Tyler pushed off the porch with his legs setting the swing into motion. "It gets pretty stressful and tiring and lonely."

"Doesn't sound all that appealing." She laughed.

Tyler looked over. Her cheeks still rolled from the giggle and her eyes flew wide with curiosity. Most days, life on the road wasn't appealing, but then—"Actually when I'm up on stage there's no better feeling. There's something about looking out into the crowd and focusing on someone who's singing right along with you. They know every word and you can see in their eyes that it means something to them. Whether it's just a memory of a good time or a loved one, it lets you know what you're doing is right." He paused. "It's the before and after that wears on you. Not to mention the politics of it all."

"I thought the before and after would be the exciting part," Sera said. "All the places you get to see."

He gave another hard push with his feet, propelling the swing backwards, then forwards again. "If I got to see them, yeah, it would be. Usually, I'm too tired to do anything before, and depending on the show, sometimes I don't get off stage until almost midnight. By the time we're all packed up and ready to go, it's well into the middle of the night and hard to fall asleep from the hype of it all. Like I said, it gets stressful and tiring after a while."

"You forgot lonely." Sera gave him a teasing nudge with her elbow.

Smiling back, Tyler said, "Yeah, it gets pretty lonely too."

"You know, there's medication to help you with stress. Also things that will help you sleep," she offered facetiously, throwing Tyler's words back at him.

"I'm well aware of the meds, but unlike you, I don't have a problem with taking them."

...

Tyler's confession surprised Sera. She turned to fully face him, to see if he was joking, and knew by the way his lips pulled tight that he wasn't. Worried that she might have offended him, she started to apologize. "Tyler, I didn't—"

"It's all right. No offense taken," he interrupted.

"What do you take?" she asked.

"Why? Are you interested in seeing if I have better stuff than you?"

She nudged him again, letting him know she'd gotten his joke. He laughed back. It was so good to hear his laugh.

"Xanax," Tyler said. "A low dose for anxiety, but I mostly take it at night to help me sleep."

"Been there and done that," she said with a shake of her head. "I'm on Celexa and Trazodone now, but they keep changing it up every few months to see what works best."

"And what works best?"

Sleeping next to you. "Nothing really."

"What happened over there, Sera?"

Tyler's voice dropped and with it, Sera's heart. She didn't want to go there. Not tonight. The day had been good for her. No meltdowns or arguments. In fact, she'd enjoyed one of the more pleasant and peaceful days she'd had in a long time and she didn't want it to end laced with bad memories.

"We've talked about me. I think tonight you should tell me what the problem is with your release."

Staring straight ahead, it took Tyler several long minutes to respond. "You've heard the song. What do you think of it?"

Although she knew the answer, she asked anyway. "So that's the song you want to release?"

"Actually no … ah." Tyler ran a hand through his thick hair. "I don't know." Crossing his arms, he continued. "I do in a way and I don't. My label is pushing it, though."

Worried that the conversation may propel them into another argument, she tried to make herself comfortable by turning in the swing to face him. Her knee brushed against his thigh as she did, sending another zap of energy surging through her.

Taking a breath, she answered. "The song is beautiful. You should release it." The words, although honest and simple, weren't easy to say. So much emotion came along with hearing that song, she didn't know where to begin.

With no movement—even the swing had stopped—Tyler stared straight ahead. "They'll release it no matter what I say. They don't need my approval. Please don't placate me with what you think I want to hear. You know what the song is about. I need to know how you're going to feel about hearing it on the radio."

So it had nothing to do with her approval or his permission at all. The song would be aired whether either one of them liked it. She at least appreciated Tyler took how she might feel about it into consideration.

She thought hard before replying again, this time trying to convey more deeply how the song affected her. "The first time I heard it, I hated it. I ejected it out of the player and was about to throw the disk on the ground and stomp it into a zillion pieces like you said, but I couldn't. Something wouldn't let me. So I listened again. I'm pretty sure the urge the second time was even stronger, but still I couldn't bring myself to get rid of it. It sat on my desk for a few days before I popped it in again. After the initial shock wore off, I was able to appreciate its beauty. I wasn't lying when I told you it's beautiful and that you should release it. I don't doubt it will be a hit."

When Tyler didn't respond and turned his face away again, silently staring off into the darkness, Sera sat confused on what maybe she did or didn't say. She'd told him how wonderful the song was despite how difficult it had been to hear. *He wanted to know how you felt.*

Clasping her hands, she looked down. Her stomach knotted. She swallowed back the vulnerability that came with releasing her feelings. "It broke my heart all over again," she said, thinking back to the heart-wrenching anguish of hearing their breakup—and how much Tyler had cared for her—played through music. The song implied he had some regrets and she wasn't sure exactly what those were, but his feelings for her had been clear. It was a permanent painful reminder of the love that she'd lost. Yet in some way, each time she heard it, the pain lessened.

Tyler turned to say something, but Sera cut him off with a raise of her hand. He'd asked and she'd started, so he was going to hear everything she had to say before she changed her mind.

"But hearing that you had felt as deeply for me as I did you was comforting. I know it's just a song and every word didn't derive from our relationship, but I hope our time together didn't leave you with a box of regret as the title states. I hope nothing I gave you or we had ended up being stuffed into a cardboard box, because there's nothing about our relationship I've ever regretted, Tyler."

CHAPTER 10

Tyler barely heard the loud thump that woke him. He hadn't been in bed long enough to drift off permanently, caught somewhere in between reliving the day with Sera and the black clouds that take over just as you let it all go. Their talk, although difficult to swallow, did give him some respite with the song's release. Hearing Sera's confession had made him sad, but happy in a way too. He'd broken her heart not once, but twice. He'd come here, trying to work through the feelings of possibly doing it a third time—and now he knew he would do anything to make sure it never happened again. Their talk had also given him hope that Sera might still feel as strongly for him as he did her.

His chest burned with excitement from seeing her eye him all day. What he liked even more was she wasn't acting shy about it. It was a glimpse of the old Sera. He missed the outgoing woman he fell in love with, but there was something captivating about the newer version too. It didn't matter which personality was standing in, the introvert or extrovert. Both sides pulled at him in a way he hadn't felt for a while.

He hadn't realized just how bad of a funk he'd been in until he'd arrived there. The exhaustion was wearing on him. Most days he preferred to stay in bed with no care or concern for what was really going on. Other than his mom and Roy, he'd lost all contact with anyone from Cobb City and the constant rounds from state to state never left much time for making new friends. He had his band mates, most of whom spent their free time with their children and wives. Jayson, his drummer, was the one person he talked to on a regular basis other than his manager, Bradley. And Bradley was far from being someone Tyler trusted on a personal level. They were from two different sides of the spectrum. They worked well together, but that was where any relationship began and ended. Tyler had pretty much been on his own for a while. He worked all the time and when he wasn't working, he was thinking about work. Other than that, he had nothing else going for him. Not even anyone to share all that he'd busted his ass for to achieve. He missed quiet dinners and watching TV. Sitting on the porch talking about the day. He even found mowing the yard and grocery shopping entertaining. Like Sera, he missed being normal. Their demons might be different, but they were fighting some of the same things.

When another loud sound came, he worried that someone might be trying to break in and got up. He looked first in the living room and kitchen, before checking both doors and the bathroom. Seeing that everything was okay, he knocked on Sera's door last. She was sitting cross-legged on the floor with an open cardboard box in front of her.

"I'm sorry, some other boxes fell out of the top of my closet when I was trying to get this one down," she explained.

"It's all right." Crossing his arms over his chest, he asked, "Need help?"

• • •

Sera looked up to see Tyler's body fill the entire door frame. Unable to fall asleep, she already recognized the spiraling down-turn of emotions that took her for a ride on nights like this. She didn't want to succumb, but didn't know how to stop it either. She wanted desperately to wean herself off the sleeping pills, but wasn't having much luck. "I couldn't sleep."

Tyler crossed the room, sprawling out lengthwise next to her on the floor. "What's in the box?"

She peeked in as if to see what it held, already knowing the few things it contained. The entire contents from her life in the army. "Mostly pictures. A Bible my mom sent when I was in Afghanistan. The St. Christopher's medal Uncle Roy gave me when I left for basic training." That piece in particular was odd, being that they weren't really affiliated with any kind of church. However the gesture meant more than its spiritual meaning. "Letters I received." There might have been a few other small items, but aside from the clothes in her closet, that was what she'd come home with.

She closed the lid and stood to put it back in its place in the closet. He rose with her.

"You don't have to put that up on my account."

"Trust me." She smiled shyly. "It's better that I do. Why aren't you playing tonight?" she asked, taking a seat on the bed.

Sera patted the spot next to her, like Tyler had done earlier in the evening when they were on the swing.

Following her instruction, Tyler settled into the mattress and leaned against the headboard. "Thought I'd give it a rest. Maybe let you get some sleep. I see that didn't work, though."

She gave a small laugh. "I don't sleep anyway. Hearing you play is actually comforting."

"I'm glad you like it." Tyler smiled.

"I always did." She took in a deep breath. "I'm proud of you, Tyler. I really am. You went after what you wanted and you did it."

"Thanks, that means a lot."

Gone was all the bitterness of the last few days. She had left it at the railroad tracks. Once she'd made the decision to do so, it was much easier to do than she'd thought. In fact, she was happy Tyler was there and not just in Cobb City. The hundred reasons why she knew having him in her bed was a bad idea were all but forgotten by the simple fact that she liked having him close. She felt safe when he was near and knew she could tell him anything. Not that she intended to start spilling her guts, but merely knowing she could trust him was comforting. She hadn't had many comforting moments since Afghanistan.

. . .

Sera woke thankful for another full night's rest. Two good nights within three days, and this time, she hadn't even woken in a panic. She felt pretty lucky until she realized that more had stirred awake than just her mind. The hard mass her body tucked into was a clear reminder of what she'd been craving. His arm snagged around her waist, fastening her to his side. She couldn't move without waking him, even if she wanted to—which she didn't.

How they'd managed to cozy up next to one another during the night, she didn't know. They'd talked for hours. Mostly about the places Tyler had been. He seemed to have a memory of every venue he'd played. She remembered some of the stories from Merv's, but he gave more in-depth details when relaying them to her now. She enjoyed hearing them, just as much as she enjoyed the silences that came in between that let her know he was getting tired, until finally his voice didn't pick up again. He'd fallen asleep first. There was no question of whether or not she'd wake him, and after covering him with a thin quilt, she slipped back in bed. Afraid of what the uncontrolled urges might tempt her to do if they were close enough to touch, she left plenty of room, ensuring it wouldn't happen.

Her subconscious demands were obvious now that it had. And whoa! It was definitely demanding. Everything seemed to rouse at once. Her hands itched to feel the roughness of his face against her palms, to smooth her thumb underneath his eyes where she knew the skin was soft. His long, thick lashes played havoc down below, reminding her just how long it had been.

Another time, another place and she would readily hurtled herself on top of Tyler and began the pleasant task of waking him with slow, torturous moves. But she and Tyler weren't what they used to be. In fact, she was finding out that they were much different than before, and instead of climbing aboard and enjoyably forcing their bodies together, she folded her head closer into Tyler's shoulder.

She hadn't realized how badly she'd missed the physical contact that only came with being in his arms. It was like she was home after being gone for so long. In a sense, she was. She was right back where she'd been before going to the army. It felt good. It felt really good, especially since she felt no obligation to lie there and cuddle with him for any reason other than because she wanted to.

Cuddling wasn't enough to bypass the quiver from the leg she'd draped over Tyler's thigh to her middle, though. How good it would feel to get lost in what Tyler could offer. At least physically. They'd always fit together perfectly. Unfortunately, she was smart enough to know that it would always be so much more between them. They could never be each other's indulgence or friends with benefits. What they'd shared was too sacred for that. Besides, at some point, those types of arrangements always filtered into a responsibility for one of the people involved. It was a situation she'd found herself in with Rollins and it was one she wasn't interested in again. She hated that their friendship had been tainted. She regretted that she'd allowed the bond they'd formed in Afghanistan to influence her scattered thoughts. Their relationship might have started off with her thinking there was more between them, but it didn't take long for her to understand that she and Rollins were nothing more than really good friends. Unfortunately Rollins hadn't appreciated her honesty when she explained that to him.

"Somebody snores."

Unaware Tyler was awake, she laughed with his words. "Yes, you do. You kept me up all night."

Tyler erupted in a chuckle. "Sweetheart, you were not up all night."

"How do you know?"

"Because I woke up a little after midnight and you were sound asleep." He smoothed her hair down against her back.

"But you still snore," she teased again, lifting her head to see him fully.

She was suddenly becoming worried about the situation. Twice they'd slept together. Maybe not in the conjugal sense, but in the same bed, and last night they'd crossed over from just a friendly gesture to something more. *Had he pulled her into his arms when he woke or had her body reacted to him being so close?* The problem was, despite what her body wanted, she didn't know exactly what kind of "more" it meant or what she could offer and if Tyler was even interested. The few hints he'd thrown didn't mean he was looking for a relationship. He could simply be lured into rekindling the past for a short fling before he set off around the country again. Either way, they needed to figure it out.

She tilted her head up to see the clock on the other side of the bed. Almost ten. She had two hours before Maggie would be there to bring her to her therapy appointment.

Tyler dropped a kiss to the top of her head when she sank back into his chest. It was friendly enough, but the way her hand rubbed underneath his shirt sleeve was much more intimate—and a line she was hesitant to cross when she realized what she was doing. The internal quandary made her stop, but she didn't pull her hand away, catching sight of the ink surrounding his arm. She pulled the hem of the sleeve up for a better view and saw her name, beautifully inscribed, staring back. It was the stupidest thing he'd ever done. She'd told him so when he got it and had even asked what he planned to do if they ever broke up and met someone else. Of course he'd laughed at her and said that it would never happen. Yeah, right, Sera thought with a nervous snort. "Bet you regret having to explain this to the ladies."

She hadn't meant to say that out loud. Biting down on her lip, she regretted it. She didn't want to know more about Tyler's personal life. Did she?

•••

Tyler looked down at his arm where Sera thumbed the black color. He could now admit that it was an eighteen-year-old spur-of-the-moment thing to do, but to this day he never regretted her name had become a permanent part of him.

He laughed dryly, trying not to cough out the swell of emotions that had woken with her in his arms. Silently, he wondered if she had any understanding of exactly what she meant to him, and how she might react to knowing that there'd been others with whom he'd tried to distract himself. Not many, but a few, and it was just that—a distraction for what he was missing with her.

"I've been asked about it a few times," he admitted honestly.

"How many?"

The snap in her voice had him taking a deep breath as he pressed his lips together. Of course Sera automatically assumed they were talking about sexual encounters, which they were, but she hadn't actually asked that. And of course it mattered to her that he'd been with others even though they'd been apart. Despite their current situation—and he wasn't even sure what that was— Sera had a jealous streak. For the most part it was flattering, but when she let her insecurities run wild, he hated trying to make her see reason. Because sometimes she was the most unreasonable person he knew.

"There's been a handful," he answered, then asked, "How about you?" So she'd know he had the right to ask if she did.

"One," Sera blurted out, rolling off his chest and sitting up.

He could see where this was going. She was on the bedside, ready to get up, before he was able to grasp her arm. Forcing her around, he asked, "Why are you mad at me?"

"I'm not mad."

"The hell you aren't. You forget how well I know you."

She shrugged from his grasp. Standing, she straightened her shirt over her shorts, snapping, "I'm not the same girl you think you know. And I'm not mad."

Shuttling to the door in record speed, she couldn't get out of the room fast enough. She was right about one thing, she wasn't the same. The Sera he knew met things head on. And while she might be trying to do that with her problems stemming from the military, she kept running away from him.

CHAPTER 11

Sera sat looking out at the hillside, noticing for the first time since being back in Cobb City how kind spring had been that year. The trees were lush with color, the ground covered in a carpet of hunter green and dark emerald. She had never seen any other place that compared to the beauty that Kentucky had to offer. Although Chicago could certainly boast about its sculpted cityscape, it held too much hustle and bustle for one to really enjoy anything it presented, and Texas, where she'd been stationed prior to and after her deployment, reminded her too much of the sandbox overseas to bring any pleasant memories. At the age of sixteen and within weeks of her arrival, she knew Kentucky would always be her home.

Hearing the door creak open and then close, she continued to stare out at the wooded slope until Tyler sat down on the steps beside her. She waited for him to say something and when he didn't, she grew tired of all the tension-filled silences of the past few days. "I'm not mad at you."

"So what happened in there, then?"

So much for giving way to all the bitterness. "Maybe I am, but not for the reasons you think."

"Why then?"

How he could be so calm when she wanted to roar, she didn't know. It was infuriating, though. She brushed her head sideways to look at him. His stoic look, trained forward, gave no real indication of his true disposition. He wasn't calm, although there was softness underneath the harsh tone in his voice. She wasn't sure what he was. So much about Tyler was different, yet the same.

"I can't believe we are even talking about this," she said, thinking about the conversation that had her flying out of the house.

"About what?"

"About sleeping with other people."

"You brought it up."

She had. "I know. I'm sorry."

"Plus, I thought you said you weren't mad about that."

"I'm not." She wasn't really. Jealous, yes. Mad, no. There was no point in being mad about something she was also guilty of. "I'm upset because you still affect me with the simplest of things. I thought we were done and I'd moved on. But clearly not as well as I thought … and I'm so damn mad at myself for feeling that way. It's maddening to know I'm still jealous over you when I have no right to be."

"You never called."

"What?" she asked, turning toward him.

"You hung up on me and never called back."

How their conversation had gone from jealousy to the day when their relationship ended, she didn't know. She didn't want to go there either. "What does that have to do with anything?"

"You must still have feelings if you're jealous."

"So you're putting all the blame on me because I never called you back?"

"I just want to know why."

Leaning forward, she rubbed her fingertips at the sides of her temples. They were getting nowhere. "I don't know why, Tyler. I don't know why I did any of it." She covered her face. "All the tension between us before I left, I knew I was doing it, but don't ask me why, because I don't know what to tell you." Dropping her head to her chest, she said, "Maybe I am crazy."

"You're not crazy, Sera."

"You don't think?" She smirked. "I came home hoping to get my life back together, and it's more of a mess now than it was two months ago. I don't know if I'm coming or going most days. One minute I can't stand you and the next I enjoy being around you. I don't want you here to remind me what a disaster I am, but then I get jealous and I sleep better when you're there. I'm confused about so many things and it's not just you. I don't understand why I'm having such a difficult time. What I went through was nothing, yet I act like it was a catastrophe."

"People react differently to situations. There isn't a textbook that tells you how you're supposed to respond. I don't know what happened, although I keep hoping you'll tell me. I do know that you need to quit beating yourself up because no matter what it was, it wasn't your fault."

"But it was."

"No," Tyler adamantly stated. "It doesn't matter to me what you maybe did or didn't do. I know you and I know that you would never have done anything that intentionally hurt anyone."

"That doesn't mean I wasn't at fault."

"I don't know what I can say here," Tyler snapped. "There's nothing I can do to make you understand that you couldn't have changed anything. Sometimes life just sucks, Sera, and I'm sorry that it sucks for you right now. Is that what you want to hear?"

"No!" she shouted. "It's not. I told you I didn't want your pity."

"Then what do you want from me?"

Trying to hide her face, she turned away, biting down on the inside of her lip. She had already cried more in the last five days than she'd done in the last year and she was tired of crying. Standing, she refused to look at Tyler when she said, "I don't want anything."

• • •

Like she'd done several times over the last couple of days, when things started getting heated, Sera left him alone to think about what she'd said. He was having trouble digesting it all, except that Sera admitted to knowing what she was doing to them prior to her deployment. If she'd known the stress she caused, then why had she continued to do it? She said she didn't know—but dammit, he didn't understand how she couldn't. Clearly something had caused her to lash out and cause tension.

Sitting where she left him, he turned every word that was just spoken over in his head. If he'd been confused before, he was even more so now. One minute he was holding her and the next they were outside arguing. His shitty days just kept getting shittier. The only positive thing about the whole episode was that by the end of the conversation, she had gained some of her strength back. At least now she was starting to fight—another hint of the old Sera, except he wished she'd pick her battles more carefully. This wasn't something they needed to argue over. They needed to talk it through.

When he heard the door open and close again, he looked over his shoulder. She'd come back out, but it was clear she wasn't there to talk. Her change of clothes into a pair of jeans and a short-sleeved top let him know she was leaving. The roar of a car pulling into the drive confirmed his suspicion. Maggie got out before Sera could descend the steps. Worried that their conversation had finally pushed her over the edge, he stood.

"Hey, Tyler." Maggie waved graciously.

He threw his head up in her direction, but couldn't bring himself to speak. It wasn't until Sera was in the yard that he finally forced his mouth open. "Sera."

She turned with her glorious warm eyes staring right back at him. The glimmer of moisture puddled in the corners let him know she was as much bothered by their talk as he.

"Ya'll going to Merv's?" It was the only thing he could think to say.

She looked at him, her face straight, lacking any sort of emotion. "I have an appointment. I'll be back later."

CHAPTER 12

Tyler heard the shower running when he came home. Knowing she'd come back like she'd promised she would strengthened his trust that they might be able to work this through. However, he was happy for the few moments alone so he could better prepare his lingering thoughts.

The bomb she'd dropped that morning was still heavy on his mind. He'd carried the blame and guilt of losing his temper and letting her go for years and now he was trying to wrap his head around the fact that Sera had known she was brewing trouble between them, whether purposely or not. Sometimes it was hard to understand what went through her head. He'd spent the day driving around the back roads of Cobb City, trying to tame his anger. He visited all the places he and Sera used to go, and ended up sitting at the railroad crossing just before the turn down the road to Roy's. He thought about the night he'd asked her to marry him. She'd been home on leave after graduating from basic training. They were barely twenty and thought they knew it all. Boy, they'd been wrong about a lot of stuff, but one thing he was still sure of: He loved her just as much now as he'd loved her then, and he was fairly confident after thinking more clearly about everything she'd said that morning that she felt the same. He just wasn't sure how any of it could work out when the problems of the past were weighted down with what she was going through in the present.

The opening of the refrigerator jostled his attention. He hadn't heard her come out of the bathroom, but the sight of her curvy hips bent over made him lose any remaining irritation. His mind went back to bed that morning. Her sleepy smile had shot straight to his groin. Had her knee rested a little farther to the left, she would have felt how just how much he'd wanted her.

A sudden throb in his jeans had him looking down to see just where his thoughts had taken him. The bulge forming between his thighs said he needed to think of something else.

"Hungry?" he asked with a light cough. "Want to go get something at Merv's?"

Sera turned, but her attention remained on the contents inside the refrigerator. "Sweet tooth. Maggie and I stopped for dinner."

"Well, then, I know exactly where we should go."

She looked at him. "The Dairy Freeze?"

He smiled.

• • •

He barely had time to pull out onto the road when he worried the turbulent day was headed south again.

"I'm sorry," she said quietly.

In a span of twelve hours they'd gone from waking up looking forward to the day ahead, to arguing, and now back to stilted conversation. Tyler's eyes slid sideways to get a good look at her, seeing that her face was soft with anticipation of what he might say in response. He'd never been good at staying angry when it came to her, and that hadn't changed. "I think we both were thrown off by seeing each other again," he said, hoping to ease some of the tension.

"Yeah." She smiled with a soft laugh. "I thought I knew what I'd do when I saw you, but it didn't happen quite like I pictured." She looked out the passenger window. "Except for the incident with your truck."

Sensing she was trying to lighten the mood, Tyler asked, "Oh really? How did you think it would go?" He threw her a wink to reinforce his disposition.

Sera laughed louder. "Ugly!" She quieted. "And a lot of yelling and cussing and me telling you what a jerk you were."

He chuckled. "Trust me. I imagined it quite the same way."

"I'm such a pain."

Tyler wasn't sure how to respond. There was something riding on the edge of her teasing charm that told him she was being more serious than he initially believed. He joked back anyway. "Yes, you are," he agreed, grinning.

"Why did you put up with me? I wasn't easy to get along with."

There was definitely a change; the soft flow of her voice let him know she wasn't trying to be comical in any way. Pulling the truck to the side of the road, he turned in his seat. Mustering up every ounce of sincerity he'd been holding inside, he said, "I never wanted easy. Easy gets boring."

She looked down at her hands.

He continued. "You kept me on my toes. Every minute I ever spent with you was worth it. Yes, sometimes you can be a pain in the ass, but with you, I never for a moment doubted that you loved me."

Sera looked up at him, the truth of what he said reflected in her eyes. Leaning in, he smoothed back the hair straddling her shoulder. He'd been to thirty-nine of the fifty states, and she was still the most beautiful woman he'd ever laid eyes on. Afraid that if he didn't take the moment she'd just handed him it may not come again, he let his hand linger behind her on the seat. "Our personalities may have been polar opposites, Sera, but loving each other was never difficult. Loving you always came easily."

He waited for a response. He thought for sure she would at least acknowledge his feelings, but nothing came as she took in a deep breath and turned toward the passenger side window. After another long minute and exhausted from the struggle to get her to open up, he pulled the truck back out onto the road.

Then he heard, "I had my first appointment at the VA with a new therapist this morning."

. . .

Sitting outside the Dairy Freeze, watching Sera spoon chocolate ice cream into her mouth, Tyler tried to figure out what was going on between them. He felt much like she'd described earlier that morning. One minute angry and annoyed, then the next dying to touch her. He was still recovering from the disappointment of her changing the subject when he'd laid out his feelings. Then to make it worse, she wouldn't even open up about the VA appointment she'd mentioned, only saying it was a required visit and that it went well. If it was just a routine appointment, then why had she brought it up? Simply because she didn't want to address her feelings? Well, if she didn't want to address hers, then why the hell had she asked about his? It was completely unfair that he kept putting himself out there without getting anything in return, yet he knew he'd do it again if she asked, because every day they spent together he saw a little more of the woman she once was.

. . .

On the drive back to Roy's, Sera thought more about her appointment at the Veterans Hospital that day. It was a requirement to obtain the medication she was almost out of. She didn't like the meds, but she couldn't sleep without some kind of help. It was the mood enhancer that bothered her most, though. It felt like a betrayal of her conscience. How was she supposed to fix her life when a magic pill made the ugliness of the world bearable? Maybe that was the point, but it only seemed like a short-term solution because when she quit taking the little problem solver, all the evil would come crawling back.

She hated to admit she'd become jaded when it came to her psychiatric care in the army. Although she knew the military provided as best as it could for the many that needed treatment, she also knew it was greatly overwhelmed and faltered all too often. Yet even with the abhorrence for the prescriptions she'd walked out with that day, somehow her visit had restored a bit of hope that maybe there was still room for progression in her case.

The appointment with Dr. Khazi was different in many ways from the no-nonsense Captain Stallinger, whom she'd seen while still enlisted. Khazi was the epitome of what she thought a therapist should look like. Her first impression after walking into his office was that he reminded her of the children's television hero Mr. Rogers. Immediately she took a liking to his relaxed and polite demeanor and felt as if she'd known him for years. She'd spent almost a year seeing Captain Gloria Stallinger, who with her tall and lean figure and lengthy brown hair that she kept pinned up to perfection looked more like she'd rolled off a fashion runway instead of a military tarmac. Never once in any of those visits had she felt a shred of the ease she found in Dr. Khazi's office. Nor did Dr. Khazi make her feel like a revolving door as she had whenever she'd seen Stallinger. The woman barely remembered her name even though they shared biweekly visits for almost twelve months. But most importantly, unlike Stallinger, Khazi had never seen combat. While most would think that it would be hard for a soldier to relate to someone who had no idea what they were going through, she found it comforting that Dr. Khazi couldn't judge her for something he knew nothing about.

Dr. Khazi asked her how she was transitioning back into being home, and so somehow they ended up speaking more in depth and for longer about Tyler than they did her military work. Sera didn't make a habit of confiding in others that often, but there was something about Dr. Khazi that made her apt to open up. He was easy to talk to and he didn't have an air about him that screamed he knew it all. Most importantly, he felt more like a friend than the enemy.

Glancing back up at the road, Sera looked over at Tyler, thinking about what Dr. Khazi suggested in regards to the distance she'd placed between them prior to her deployment. The issue was bound to come up again after the morning's talk and she hoped that Tyler would be able to find some understanding in what she was only now starting to comprehend herself.

CHAPTER 13

Tyler stopped the truck at the signal of the approaching train. The flashing red lights had him shifting the gear in reverse, but before he could get the truck backed up, Sera placed a hand on his arm, forcing him to stop.

"Tyler. I need to do this."

He sighed. "Not tonight, Sera."

Scooting over into the middle of the seat, she placed her hand higher up on his bicep. "Please."

He stared at her, and she stared back. Finally, with a twist of his mouth, he nodded in agreement.

Sera's legs shook as the train whistle blew. Her arms shivered with a chill as she wrapped them around her aching middle. Burying her face into Tyler's shoulder, she tried to think of anything other than that awful moment back in Afghanistan. Palm trees, the blue crystal waters of the ocean, a meadow filled with brightly colored flowers. None of it helped because none of the images lasted. Her mind was like a View-Master, constantly changing pictures with a click of a button, except that the only button was the train that triggered her memories.

Tyler murmured in her ear, "Sera, baby, talk to me. Don't think about it. Remember good things."

She forced her face deeper into the opening of his arm, trying to concentrate on the sound of his low voice.

"Honey, it's all in your head. Listen to me. Think of all the good times we had out here."

Closing her eyes even tighter, she tried to fight the images, wishing she could talk because she wanted so badly to tell Tyler everything in that moment. She couldn't, though; it was as if her voice had been ripped out. The fear of what was in her head too much to bear.

"I'm here. I'm here for as long as you need me … remember that time I brought you home late and Roy made us wash his car as punishment? I was so mad at my mom for agreeing with him. Though seeing you soaking wet was pretty erotic for a seventeen-year-old."

Feeling Tyler's warm breath spraying across her ear, she fought the blackness. She wanted to go where Tyler's voice could take her. Good memories. Happier times. A place that if she ever got the chance to go again, she'd do whatever it took to accept it openly.

However, it was the smell of smoldering plastic mixed with the tartness of gun powder that won the struggle in her head. The blistering patches of black intermingled with the streaks of red running down Rollins's face were all she could think about. The long minutes of seeing his mangled body pinned helplessly under the truck made time feel as if it had stalled. She cried, screaming out for help, all the while thinking it was too late. Smearing the grime around his face, trying to get a clearer picture of what she was dealing with, she finally saw Rollins's eyes move and in that moment a gush of relief came. She really thought it was going to be okay.

It wasn't.

His physical injuries healed. The charred skin on his face was restored to barely a blemish. The dislocated shoulder was put back in place. The broken leg made a full recovery. But it wasn't the physical wounds that haunted her. They were merely a symbol for the damages she couldn't see. Rollins lived. At least he woke up and breathed air in each day. But she wasn't sure one was really alive if they did little more than open their eyes. His last few months in the army had been painful. Knowing he was getting out, he didn't bother to show up for work. Most days when she visited he hadn't showered or bathed and she could usually tell by the volume of beer bottles lying around how his day had gone. He isolated himself in his bedroom, staring off at the television, but she was sure he never absorbed anything he saw. He might have woken up each day, but he wasn't really there. At least, not as the man he was before Afghanistan.

Finally pulling out of the darkness, she sank further into Tyler's arms, burying her head deeper into his side. She wasn't shaking, nor was she thinking about the train that was now gone. She thought solely of Rollins and what he'd become.

Swallowing back a breath to level the oxygen she'd been denying the rest of her body, she swiped back the hair that had fallen around her face. There weren't any tears to dry, although she felt the pressure of them building behind her lids. She blinked several times to relieve the heaviness, and after a few seconds, with confidence that the dam wouldn't unleash, she looked up. Tyler reminded her of the boy he was years ago: gentle and caring, yet full of a powerful desire that knew exactly how to drive her crazy.

"Thank you," she said, clearing her throat.

"I'm proud of you," he whispered against her forehead before pressing his lips to her skin.

Her insides sizzled as his warm breath pulled her in again. As tempted as she was to reach up and return the kiss, she didn't want to use Tyler as a distraction from the guilt of Rollins. Besides, she was ready to address the root of their past problems before she lost the courage to do so.

"I was scared, Tyler." A soft cry came as she spoke the words that were nearly harder to admit than anything she'd ever done in her life. "I was barely twenty-one and scared to death. I know you're going to say that doesn't sound like me, but it was. I didn't want to go over there. I was so afraid and I didn't know how to tell you that."

"I was scared too." He brushed another kiss against the side of her face.

"I know you were. Which only made it worse. I worried about you worrying about me. If that makes any sense. I couldn't handle the idea of not ever seeing you, Roy, or my mom again. I didn't purposely set out to cause trouble for us. I just know every time we talked, it got harder and harder hanging up because it meant one less day I might have. It was easier to say goodbye when I was angry."

"Sera." Tyler took her face in his hands.

She tried to look away. She didn't want to see the gentleness pouring out of his eyes. She'd hurt him, years ago, and again over the past few days. It seemed to be a cycle she couldn't break and she didn't deserve his empathy. "Please don't make this easier for me."

He pulled her face back up to him, rubbing away the moisture collecting in the corners of her eyes. "What's wrong with things being easy?"

She heaved in a deep breath, unable to come up with a practical answer. There was nothing wrong with it; it was just something she didn't feel like she deserved at the moment. Opening her mouth to say so, her words were smothered away when Tyler's lips found hers. The kiss was slow, fulfilling, and every bit as satisfying as she remembered.

When it ended, they both pulled back, staring at each other. The line she'd been so hesitant to cross was gone. Turning back and trying to hide from her feelings would only tarnish the progress she and Tyler had made in putting the past behind them. It would also do nothing but leave her with regret and what-ifs later on. She didn't want to confuse or hurt him any more than she already had, though. "I don't know what I can give you right now."

Tyler's eyes never wavered when he responded back. "I'm not asking you to give me anything. I just want the chance to get back what was meant to be mine."

CHAPTER 14

Sera sat in the porch swing, enjoying another well-rested night of sleep. She was becoming spoiled when it came to sharing a bed with Tyler, even if there wasn't anything sexual going on. Something about him being there brought her comfort—let her know she wasn't fighting this on her own. And somehow that made the fight less of a struggle.

She watched as he washed his truck, laughing to herself. The truck was so ridiculously big, even for a man his size, he had to stretch and tiptoe to reach many areas. She wasn't sure what the oversized load was trying to make up for. It had nothing to do with his ego or the lack of anything down below, because he was perfect where both of those were concerned. Maybe it had something to do with pride. Like he said, he didn't get to enjoy much of anything he'd worked for, except this truck.

He was babying it today. He'd already vigorously scrubbed the tires, leaving the white wheels beaming as brightly as his teeth when he flashed a grin. She hated to tell him that as soon as he drove ten feet, the dust from the gravel would cover it right back over, but then she supposed that wasn't important. He was relaxed and seemed to enjoy what he was doing and that was all that mattered. Deciding that if he didn't have help, he'd be at it all day, she went to get an extra sponge.

The water was cool as she dipped her hand into the bucket, and then began working the soapy mess in circles around the fender. Sliding her gaze sideways, she watched the muscles in his arms tighten as he moved around beside her. "I know why you're washing your truck today."

Tyler squatted, swiping his hand from side to side on the lower portion. "Because it's a pretty day and it needs a good cleaning."

"No, because of what you said last night."

He stopped what he was doing, standing up straight. "What did I say?"

The front of his shirt was damp with suds. Dark rings emphasized his chest underneath. "You were thinking about us washing Roy's car."

A curl of pleased recognition fanned his lips. "So you were listening to me?"

She'd heard part of it, anyway. Unable to remember when she stopped hearing Tyler's voice and began seeing Rollins's face, she wasn't sure she'd absorbed it all. She sure hoped she hadn't missed him recounting what their punishment for coming home late had accomplished. "I remembered you starting the story," she answered.

Going back to his task, he dipped his sponge back in the water and began scrubbing another area. "Is that what you were thinking about while you were sitting on the porch staring at me?" He threw her a wishful grin.

Yes, she was; every clear detail. Their first time together wasn't a painful memory. Well, there was a little discomfort, but she much preferred to think of it as a beautifully raw act. Magical came to mind, because the ending had felt very magical, but magic wasn't real and the memory of what it felt like for Tyler to press into her with ease for the first time was very real. Gentle and understanding when she asked him to take it slower, she couldn't imagine sharing that experience with anyone else.

"I was," she admitted, the fluttering low in her belly back. It was the reason she'd gotten up in the first place, needing something to distract her from making love to Tyler in her head. And what did she do? Start talking to him about it. *Smooth, Sera, smooth.*

"So you remember this ..."

The cold jetted spray to her face was so unexpected she had no words at first, but then let out, "That was cold," with a giggle before scurrying to retaliate. She didn't even make it to the bucket before he grabbed her hands, clutching them behind her back.

"Oh, no, you don't," he said.

She twisted, trying to shrug out of his grasp. He tightened his hold, trapping her with his arms.

"You remember where this got you before, don't you?" he asked with a smirk. She definitely remembered: wet from the inside out. "Let go!" she yelled. The twisting and turning did her no good. He overpowered her easily.

Tyler chuckled with pleasure. Sera wriggled her hips back and forth, trying to bend out of his grip. Her face, although strung with intent, teased with a sparkle. She asked him to release her, all the while laughing as she did. The sound only encouraged him to pull her tighter, until her back was planked up against the door of his truck. Stepping in, he trapped her. With nowhere to go, her gaze soared up to meet his.

The shock of the cold water might be able to explain the tips of her nipples straining through her shirt, but she had no defense for the wanton look blazing out of her eyes. His hands fell around her backside and even in the loosened grip, she didn't move. He picked her up, not needing to coax her legs around his waist. Her arms swung around his neck and suddenly they were living in the past. Eight years prior with raging hormones.

The ridge in his shorts jolted to attention. Stretching, it implored to plunge into the apex of her thighs, already feeling the warm encompass it would offer. "You're so beautiful," he murmured, nudging in deeper.

Her breath heavy, Sera clung to Tyler's shoulder, thankful for the support he and the pickup provided. Her calves were lithe—she couldn't have stood if she wanted to—but her hips were taut with energy. She cupped the hardness pressed firmly against her thin shorts. The flexing and writhing came automatically. His body had an effect on her she couldn't control. Needing more, she surrendered. Lips parted, she tilted her face up and took his mouth. It was if he was waiting for it. He wanted her permission to move forward, but from the moment their tongues met, he took back over control. Dipping and teasing, leaving her panting for air every time his mouth moved down to her neck, nibbling at the sensitive area on her shoulder. His hands toyed with the swells rising through her shirt. She gasped. He moaned. And then the sound of a car door made them jump out of their sexual trance.

"Dammit," Tyler said under his breath.

She felt his hard point slide up her stomach coming to a rest just below her breastbone as he let her glide to her feet. They'd been so engrossed in their tryst they hadn't heard the car coming up the drive.

Legs quivering, she gained her bearings, letting Tyler tend to the visitor—or visitors, she assumed, when she heard several immature giggles all at once.

"I'm sorry to bother you, but my mom said she thought you were staying here and we were wondering if you would sign our CDs."

Sera gave the squeaky-voiced teenage girl credit for her bravery. She was also thankful that the carload had interrupted when they had. A few more minutes and clothes would have been flying in the front yard. Suddenly feeling a chill from the dampness clinging to her body, she stepped out around the truck, gave Tyler a wave, and left him with his adolescent fans.

•••

Not once since he'd started singing had Tyler not wanted to stop what he was doing to sign a few autographs. That was, until the carload of teenagers interrupted his and Sera's rendezvous. Annoyed to the point of anger, his first reaction had been to pick up a rock and chuck it their way, hoping they'd take the hint and disappear. However, they weren't skittish animals who would run off with the gesture. They were humans. Young humans, who had spent their money—or maybe their parents' money, considering how young they were—on his album. No, they shouldn't have invaded his privacy, but after fifteen minutes spent taking pictures and signing everything from their shirts, hats, and CD covers, he was glad they had.

He and Sera had been on the verge of losing total control. Not that he cared, except he didn't have condoms and had no idea if Sera was still on the pill, and he was certain that neither would have mattered if it came to that point. He would have taken her right then. And they didn't need a little baby Creech added into this already tangled mess. So instead of going in and picking up where they left off, when his company left, he went back to washing his truck.

But an hour later, as he put up his bucket and went inside, he could still taste every sweet twirl of her tongue, could feel every parting welcome of her hips. The desire to make love to her was consuming. Every time he looked at or touched her, he felt his groin stiffen and while he was ready, he wasn't sure she was. Her body might have thought so, but her mind was still trying to process what was happening between them and the last thing he wanted her to have was regrets.

She was sitting on the couch with her phone to her ear when he went inside. He got a drink, then, seeing she was still in the same position, although not talking and just listening, he went to get cleaned up. She hadn't moved when he returned. Her mouth didn't look like it had even opened in the half hour that he'd been gone. She wasn't mad or happy. She looked bored more than anything. The roll of her eyes as he went to the kitchen confirmed his suspicions.

Grabbing a pizza from the freezer, he was opening the box when she came in after finishing her call.

"How is Sylvia?" he asked, knowing she was talking to her mom.

"Good," she answered, hopping up on the countertop next to the stove.

"Good as in good or good as in the same?"

"Actually, she's doing all right. Same man for over a year now and she's still working in the office at the insurance company."

"That is good." He popped the pizza in the oven, then went to stand between her legs. Holding onto her waist, he said, "I'm beat."

"Those girls wear you out?" she asked, pressing her hands to his cheeks, massaging the skin underneath his eyes.

The warmth from her palms had him humming with need again. He tried distracting the reaction by focusing on the conversation. "There was a guy too, just so you know." He tilted his head down, teasing her with a curl of his lips.

"I'm not jealous of some teenagers," she said.

"No?"

"Nope." She shook her head, smiling.

"Good," he recounted, opening the oven door to check inside. When he glanced back up, he caught a distant look on her face. "Everything okay?"

"Yeah."

"You got that look."

"What kind of look is that?"

She wrinkled her nose up in this cute little way that had him moving to stand between her legs again. "The kind that usually means something's wrong." Except she wasn't acting like anything was amiss—her thighs trapped him, her core pressing against the bulk of him.

"I was just thinking that I never thanked you for the tickets."

If her arms weren't clasped around his neck, he probably would have stepped back. The mentioning of the one time he'd reached out to try to make right of the past cut to him sharply. Struggling to remain unnerved, he dropped his gaze to her lap. "Did you go?"

...

The apprehension of where their conversation might lead marred Tyler's face. Sera disliked the way he automatically assumed they'd float back into disharmony whenever something of their past was mentioned, but that honestly hadn't been her plan. She was trying to do right for once and the tickets had been weighing on her for a while. "I didn't, but I should have at least sent a thank-you note or something."

He stepped out of her arms to check the pizza, but didn't return when he saw it still had a few minutes to go. She already felt a loss, and wanted him back. The reaction was completely crazy, being that they were still relatively new to what was going on between them, but since the mood was set, she decided to delve further. "Why did you send them?"

He leaned against the counter, staring down at the floor. "I was in Texas. You were in Texas. It seemed like a good idea."

He shrugged as if it weren't a big deal, but it was. Whether it was what happened outside earlier or the ease of which they'd fallen back into acting like a couple, she suddenly felt as if something needed to be said or asked. She just wasn't sure what.

Letting him tend to their dinner, she didn't speak again until he was almost done slicing the pizza. "I couldn't go." Giving her a quick glance, he grabbed two plates, seeming to know what she was talking about. "I had just gotten back and I was a mess. I couldn't have dealt with you then."

Putting a piece on each plate, he pushed one toward her, then took his stance back up against the counter, this time crossing his ankles and arms. His forehead scrunched up in concern, and she knew when he opened his mouth, nothing good was going to come out.

"Maybe if you had dealt with me then, or even taken my call three years ago, we wouldn't be having this conversation right now."

Nope, definitely not what she wanted to discuss, but at least they weren't yelling, although the somber tone in Tyler's voice made her heart ache. "For the record, I didn't ignore your call. I had to report to formation. By the time it was over, you'd already left the voicemail."

Her stomach curdled in response to the gulp of air that she saw slide down his throat as his eyes cast to the side. The pain of seeing him struggle was overwhelming.

"So you would have answered if you'd been there when I called back?"

Her throat ran dry. "Yes."

The anguish too much, she jumped down and stood behind him when he turned around and pressed his hands into the countertop. "Hey," she offered, hoping to release some of the tension.

"Damn." He shook his head. "I thought the timing of the last week has been shitty, but it was pretty fucking shitty years ago too."

Unable to pull back his arm to force him to face her, she wedged herself in between him and the counter, laying her hands against his chest. "Come on, let's not do this. I didn't mean to start an argument."

His head dropped to hers. He pulled her in tight. "We aren't arguing. I'm just pissed. Pissed that my future was determined because of a missed phone call."

When he put it like that, it didn't seem fair. She wondered how differently things might have been, had she been there when he called. She would have realized how difficult she'd been and then apologized for it and they would have made up. There was a good possibility that with Tyler still in the picture, she and Rollins wouldn't have grown as close as they had. If she'd had Tyler to lean on, she wouldn't have relied so much on Rollins and then maybe things would be different for him too. So much was contingent on that one missed phone call. It was as if her life had changed in that very moment.

"Hey," Tyler said, thumbing tears out of her eyes that she didn't know were there. "It's all right. I just …"

He was as lost for words as she. He circled his arms around her and they stood, taking the quiet of the room in, both struggling with what to say next.

"I thought you would come back," he finally let out.

"What do you mean?"

"I never expected not to hear from you again."

She blinked, trying to keep the tears at bay. "You told me it was over."

"Actually." He ran his finger over her bottom lip. "I said maybe we both needed a break."

"Same thing."

"Not really, but it doesn't matter because I never meant it."

"What did you mean to happen, then?"

"Honestly?" He let out a sigh. "I thought you'd fight for me. For us."

She laughed. "So you broke up with me thinking I'd come running back to you? That's a little pretentious, don't you think?"

"No. I thought you'd at least give me a piece of your mind, though, and then it would just work itself out like it always had before."

How many times she'd thought about doing just that. Writing a letter or giving a call, but she could never put the words to paper or force herself to pick up the phone. It was as if the idea of fighting in a war drained her desire to fight for anything else.

"My mind was already thousands of miles away. I was dealing with what I would be faced with over there. I didn't have the strength to fight for you."

"I know," he said, his face dipping down for a kiss. "I realize that now, and I'm sorry. I should have fought harder for you."

CHAPTER 15

Sera looked on hesitantly as Tyler hitched Roy's boat to his truck. Her uncle had some peculiarities; his lawn and his boat were two of them. She didn't think Roy would approve of them taking the boat out and she really didn't want to start off on his bad side when he got back from Florida if something should happen.

"Tyler, I really don't think this is a good idea."

He simply gave her a look that that implied she was raining on his parade. He'd woken up excited about fishing that morning. She was thrilled with the idea too—that was, until she realized he planned to take the boat.

"You know how he is with his boat."

"Yeah, I know." He ignored her warnings, continuing to secure the boat to his truck.

"You should call him."

"Sera, it's okay. Using his boat is one of the perks that comes along with being his stepson."

Climbing in the truck, she had nothing more to say. Tyler started the thunderous motor, roaring the engine to life. The sound was completely out of place in the quietness of the holler, yet she paid little attention as the idea of Roy and Tyler now related— although not by blood—seemed even more awkward.

Finally as they maneuvered down the gravel road, she said, "You know that makes us step-cousins, don't you?" She cocked her head and smiled, waiting to see what he might say in return.

Giving a cheesy grin, he replied, "Kissing cousins?"

"That's gross," she threw back.

"Well, we are in Kentucky."

She wrinkled her nose at the thought. "Kind of weird, though, isn't it? I mean your mom and him?"

"Not really. They spent a lot of time together because of us. It doesn't surprise me. I saw it coming."

Roy was still on her mind when they got out onto the water. Her uncle, even with his gruff stance on life, and oddities, was the kindest soul she'd ever met. He was the only father figure she'd ever known. Yet he'd been so much more than that. Some people had single moms or dads. She had a single uncle, whom she was certain had saved her from a life destined for destruction.

"I'm glad they have each other," she said, happy that Diana appreciated her uncle's quirks.

"Huh?" Tyler asked as he cast his line deep out into the lake.

"Your mom and Roy … I'm glad they're together."

• • •

Tyler craned his neck to look back at Sera. Perched up on the bench seat at the back of the boat, she showed off her trim arms with an orange tank top, which she'd rolled up, allowing the sun to reflect off the five inches of golden skin just below her breast to the edge of her hips. For a moment, he forgot about what he was doing. The woman was driving him insane. Not only emotionally, but physically too. He thought more than once last night about finding an excuse to run into town to buy protection. Having to sleep next to her with the memory of their encounter from earlier in the day still on his mind tormented him in every imaginable way. He was thick with need when they slipped into bed and then had woken in the same manner that morning. If their bodies met again like they had while washing his truck, he wasn't sure he'd have the willpower to pull back if she was willing to go further. If it did happen, he wanted to be prepared for it, which was why he was running by the store on the way home.

"I mean, I don't want him to be alone for the rest of his life."

He continued to stare, not paying much attention to what she said. Long strands of hair wisped around her face, and her hand smoothed them back only for it to happen again. With one leg bent up toward the sky and the other stretched out straight, she looked perfectly happy.

"And I like your mom. She was good to me, kind of like having another mom in a way."

He really wanted to cover her body with his and to smother her obsessive chatter away with a kiss.

"Tyler, are you even listening to anything I'm saying?"

The high-pitched sound of her voice directed his attention from her legs to her face, which was staring prudently at him.

He chuckled. "Not really. You're breaking the rules. Remember? Besides, we're supposed to be fishing, not flapping our jaws."

She stuck her tongue out and stood, baiting her hook. "How am I breaking the rules?"

"We agreed not to talk about anything bad or in the past today. It's supposed to be a good day."

"Roy and your mom are in the present, not the past."

She had him. In more ways than one. Sliding over, he leaned in, nuzzling her neck with his mouth. "You're right. No rules broken, you win."

"What do I win?" She laughed.

"This." He kissed her. Hard. Unrelentingly and feverously. He poured every kiss he'd missed the last three years into it, working their mouths together, tangling his fingers through her hair as he did.

"I like winning," she said, smiling when he pulled back.

• • •

By late afternoon, they'd caught at least a dozen fish between them. Sera hid a mischievous grin every time she pulled one in bigger than Tyler's. It was an unspoken challenge of who could outdo the other and one that they both took seriously. That was, until she looked over and found him staring intently off into the water waiting for a tug on his line. His determined stance made her lose interest in the game. She put down her pole and sat balled up on the seat, content to watch him for the rest of the day.

The sheer sunlight cast a pink glow across his chest, contrasting the barely visible white line that peeked out from the khaki shorts riding low on his waist. He'd regret not wearing sunscreen tomorrow, but the bronzing he would receive as a result would probably help even out the two tones on his arms. Not that it mattered to her. She liked him just as he was.

She liked all of him, not just his looks. His humble personality was equally attractive as the side of him that never faltered in making her laugh. In so many ways he was still the same Tyler that she'd fallen in love with all those years ago. Yet in many ways he'd changed too. She hated to say that he'd grown a temper, but he had, in a good kind of way. No longer was he the passive boy who never wanted to fight. He'd matured into a man who didn't settle for anything less than what he wanted—and he'd made it clear he wanted her. Or at least a chance to see if they still had any kind of future together. She'd love nothing more than to see that happen, but she also had worries of living up to the woman he remembered. Because like him, she knew she'd changed too.

"Like what you see?"

His sexy drawl forced her eyes back up to his face. She grinned at the idea of being caught ogling him. "Of course."

Reeling in his line, he set it aside and took a seat next to her, pulling her close when he stretched out and crossed his ankles. Basking in the warmth of the day, they sat like that for a long time, enjoying the soft rock of the boat, with neither saying anything. It was a comfortable silence, unlike those that plagued them just a few days ago. For the first time in months, she felt completely relaxed. There wasn't any pressure to think about getting her life together or worries that something might go wrong. It was just her and Tyler and nothing else but the afternoon sun.

"I've missed this," Tyler said after a few moments.

Sucking in a breath of fresh air, she turned her head up toward the sky. "Me too. I can't remember the last time I went fishing." She considered when Tyler's last time fishing might have been, wondered how often he really made time for himself.

Tyler imitated her actions, looking up into the sunlight, then leaned in, nudging her shoulder. "I'm not just talking about fishing. The peace and quiet and being here with you." Moving his hand through her hair, he turned down to nuzzle her face her again. "I've missed you, Sera. I mean, really missed you. I know we already talked about what happened, but just because we weren't together didn't mean that I wasn't thinking about you. 'Cause I did, every day."

She lifted her head, trying not to get caught up in the swell of emotions swirling through the air. Shading her eyes, she answered back, "I missed you too. But ..." She leaned back into his embrace "I think you need to make more time for yourself."

"That's kind of hard to do right now."

"What's so hard about it?"

"When you have responsibilities, you have to take care of them."

"Maybe you should cut back on your responsibilities, then."

"Again, that's easier said than done, sweetheart."

"I don't see that it is."

"It is when I have people telling me I need to go here or go there. I can't just say no."

"Then tell the *people* that you need to relax."

"Somehow I don't think they'd quite understand. It's a business. It's about making money."

She straightened, pulling a bent knee into the seat. "Aren't you the boss, though?"

He laughed. "Sort of … not really. I may not be an employee per se, but I still have people who are in charge of my career who I have to answer to."

"But don't you choose those people? I mean your manager, publicist, everyone else. You hire them, right?"

"I do."

"So what's the problem?"

"They do what's best for me and I have to trust them and do what they say."

Seeing they were talking in circles, she let out a sigh, then asked, "Can I ask you something?

"Sure."

"Did you start singing for the money?"

"You know I didn't."

"Then why is it important to push yourself past the point of exhaustion just to make a dollar?"

"It's not about the money."

"Then what's it about?"

"Letting people down and not giving my all to those that believed in me."

"So it's the people responsible for your career that you're worried about?"

"Yes."

"Well, I think you need to find new people, then. Whether they opened up doors for you or not, you need someone who understands what's important to you. Killing yourself isn't important."

He laughed again. "Maybe I need you in charge of my career."

"Oh no," she said. "That would be a disaster."

"All right, well then, let me ask you something."

"What?"

"If you hadn't gone into the army, what would you have done?"

"Honestly?"

"Of course."

"Probably worked at Merv's until your career took off, then gone wherever you were at."

It was a moment before he responded and she worried maybe she'd fallen back into the ease of their relationship too easily. She was starting to talk without weighing her words and found herself saying things that a week and a half ago she never would have thought about saying.

Then he asked, "Would you consider it now?"

Startled with the question, she looked away, but didn't hesitate to answer. "I can't right now, Tyler."

"Why not?"

"Because I have too much going on."

"Whether you're here or with me, that's not going to change."

"No, it's not," she said. "But you don't need me tagging along right now. You've got enough to worry about."

"And you think I'm not going to worry about you when I leave? At least if you were with me, I'll know how you're doing."

"Tyler," she pleaded. "Trust me on this. I'm not ready."

Another silence followed. Worrying that Tyler might sink back into the strain of the past week and hoping to deflect the tension, she stood, picking her pole up. "You're the one breaking the rules now."

He followed her lead, slinging his arm out widely. The lure glided through the air and drop into the water. *So much for having a good day.*

CHAPTER 16

"Ouch," Tyler barked.

"Sit still."

"Quit being so rough."

Tyler's back arched when the glop of cold aloe vera gel ran down his scorched flesh. He winced when Sera's hands began to work in circles, lathering up the ointment.

"I'm not being rough. I told you to put on sunscreen."

She'd known as soon as they got home yesterday that he would be paying for his lack of skin protection. He carried his pale complexion well, but the bright rays of the sun had never been his friend.

"Sunscreen is for pansies."

"Sunscreen is for people who don't want skin cancer or wrinkles."

"Darlin', you're going to get wrinkles anyway. It's called old age and we are all going to die someday."

"Maybe so," she answered, grazing her fingertips over his velvet colored shoulders. "But why hurry the process or make it worse? There," she said with the click of the lid. "Can we go now? I'm ready for another day enjoying the outdoors."

Holding on to the sidebar of the Kubota with a death grip, Sera's body jostled from side to side along the rough narrow path. The long sleeves she wore did nothing to inhibit the briar bushes from attaching her arms, but at least her legs were safe inside the all-terrain vehicle. The vibration of her head against the back of the seat as they ascended up a small hill made her wonder why on earth she'd once thought riding the old logging trails behind Roy's house was fun. That was, until the bumpy road turned into one of the many hidden beauties of the Bluegrass State: an open pasture filled with leafy green grass and blossoming white and yellow wild flowers.

With a bottle of water, she and Tyler sat on top of a large boulder, taking a break. The fresh air was a godsend after the dust from the trail, as was the slight breeze that blew giving some reprieve to the warm temperature—also indicating that the weatherman was correct. Rain showers were moving in, not that the already flourishing foliage needed any. The vibrant colors of summer were in bloom all around.

Twisting the lid back on her bottle, she looked up at the sky, searching for more proof of the incoming weather. Aside from a few cotton-colored clouds mingling together, nothing stood out. Although she was trying not to think about it, the talk the day before had cemented the fact that Tyler's time was winding down. Nothing permanent other than she wasn't going with him had been discussed. The possibility of leaving with Tyler wasn't something she'd considered when she decided to give this romance a second chance. Actually there was no choice to be made. Long distance for now was all that she could give. It was a situation that scared her, though, because the separation had been tough for them before.

"So where does the tour kick off?" she asked, dangling her feet against the oversized rock.

"Charlotte."

"Are you excited?"

"Yeah, I am, but it's also a lot of work. I'll be worn out by the time February comes."

"You'll be home for Christmas, right?"

Tyler threw her a teasing grin. "Missing me already?"

"Actually I am." Although fully clothed, saying things like that made her feel as if she were stark naked.

"Then come with me."

She took in a sharp breath, unable to blame anyone but herself for opening the door to that again. Unfortunately, this time she couldn't use the excuse of breaking rules to change the subject. "You know I can't do that."

"Not really. I don't understand what's stopping you."

Sliding off the side of the rock, she crossed her arms and ankles and leaned back. "I have appointments, for one."

"We'll make sure you're home for the appointments."

She let out a deep breath. What happened to things being easy? "It's not just about the appointments."

Tyler jumped down next to her. The empty water bottle in his hand wound up tightly into a spiral. "Is it about not trusting me, then?"

Irritated that he'd brought up trust as an issue, she straightened her shoulders. "You wouldn't be sleeping in my bed if I didn't trust you."

He matched her stare, the disdain in his voice clear. "We aren't exactly sleeping together, though."

She needed no reminder that they weren't having sex. Every night as she stretched out next to him and every morning as she woke with him by her side, her body informed her of its frustrations.

"Is this how it's going to be?" she snapped back.

"How what's going to be?"

"We spend the last few days fighting over every stupid little thing?"

He leaned back. His jaw set tight as he ground his teeth together. "Are you going to tell Roy?"

She turned, planting a shoulder against the rock, knowing exactly what he was asking. "No. And you're not going to either."

"Does your mom know?"

"No," she spat, growing frustrated.

"How much have you told Maggie?"

"Nothing." Sera looked down at the ground. "She thought my appointment was a routine physical exam. Something the army requires when you get out."

"What about anybody you served with? Do you keep in contact with any of them?"

Rollins popped into her head. She hadn't heard from him for almost ten months. But not a day went by he didn't seep into her mind. "Most are getting ready to redeploy or have been transferred somewhere else. Some have gotten out and we've lost touch."

"So you have no one."

He made it sound terrible. As if she was all alone without a friend in the world. Which she was, in a way. Except for him, and he was leaving. "I do just fine by myself."

He smirked with annoyance. "Really, Sera? Fine? I don't think sitting out by a railroad track freaked the hell out is fine."

His point made, she flamed with irritation that he'd done so with such a low blow. Hands on her hips, she shouted, "What do you want me to say, Tyler? I'm lost here, but I'm trying. If I leave with you now, I'd drive us both crazy. You can't babysit me and that's what you'd want to do. I can't drive, I barely sleep. You want to drag me out on the road with you and deal with all of that when you already have so much stress in your life? No, thanks! I've already messed up one person's life. I'm not going to be responsible for another."

• • •

Tyler watched Sera walk away. Swearing underneath his breath, he yelled, "Hey, where are you going?" When she didn't stop, he ran to catch up. "Where are you going?"

She didn't turn. "Home."

"Stop. Talk to me."

Her stride never broke as she climbed into her seat. Tired of all the stifled talks just to keep peace, he leaned against the side with his shoulder, waiting until she was settled, then asked, "What do you mean, you can't drive?"

So much was starting to make sense, yet it didn't. The walking back and forth to town, the using the push mower. She'd even told him she'd sold her car, which seemed silly since she hadn't bought a new one.

"Answer me," he demanded, when she turned her face away

Still nothing. The agitation he felt from his first few days back in Cobb City came barreling back. He thought they'd surpassed all the secrets. "What do you mean, you can't drive, Sera?"

When she still refused to look at him, he lost his patience and slammed both fists down on the top of the Kubota. She jumped at the sound, but said nothing. "Talk to me, dammit!"

Her face finally met his, and a river of silent tears ran steadily down each flushed cheek. Even through the anger of being ignored, his gut twisted. Raking a hand through his hair, he rounded the front of the vehicle and got in. He knew not being able to drive was directly related to the incident in Afghanistan. Swallowing back his anger, he said, "I've been waiting for you to tell me, but I'm not sure that's ever going to happen, so I'm asking. What happened over there?"

Sera wiped at her face, corralling the tears as she sniffed back the emotions she'd let loose. For a few moments, Tyler wasn't sure she would answer, but then when she quieted, she finally did.

"We were on security duty. Rollins and I were in front leading the way," she wept.

He sat quietly listening, waiting for her to go on, all the while also considering who Rollins was. Obviously someone she served with, but man or woman, enlisted or superior? And was Rollins the one she'd been involved in the accident with?

"We had to ride around the perimeter of the town we were in. It was an easy task. In the eleven months we'd been there, there hadn't been any threats and no reason to worry. They tell you never to get too comfortable or let your guard down, but all of us had."

She paused, choking back more tears. "We started our normal route. Stopped to talk to some of the locals before continuing on. The sun was so bright that day. I told Rollins that I couldn't wait to see snow again and he laughed because I had mentioned how much I hated the winters in Kentucky. Then we started talking about what we planned to do on leave when we got back to the States." Swiping at her face again, she went on. "I never noticed how deserted the area along the railroad tracks was until it was too late. But I looked around and it became apparent just when a loud whistle blew." Sera stopped again, heaving in a deep breath. "I thought a train was coming." She looked off to the side. "No trains ever passed through there, though."

Covering her eyes with her hands, she said, "There was never a train. I guess I imagined the whistle."

Tyler listened as Sera's cries turned into a soul-ripping howl. The conversation he'd patiently waited to have for more than a week was harder to bear than he'd imagined. He shook his head, rubbing his hand over his face. Needing some comfort to soothe his own aching emotions, he reached out to take her hand, but she folded them together in her lap.

"I remember every painstaking detail," Sera continued. "When the blast went off, the pressure of my jaw smashing up into the roof of my mouth was so excruciating. Each of my eardrums felt as if they were being gouged with the tip of a knife at the same time. It was like someone was driving screws down into the top of my head. Those are just the immediate sensations—when the shock of it begins to subside, it's the lung-clogging smoke that makes you think you're dying."

Tyler finally found his voice. "But you were okay?"

Sera shook her head, but let out a small, dry laugh. "I thought I was dead. I couldn't see anything, my face was so filled with dust and grime. I didn't know the truck was on its side until I unbuckled my seatbelt and fell down into the passenger seat. I figured the pain I felt in my side as I hit meant I wasn't dead." She tried to laugh again, but it came out weak.

"What about Rollins?" Tyler asked.

Sera cleared her throat, staring straight ahead as if she were reliving the accident in her mind. "He was thrown from the truck and somehow got pinned underneath."

"He was okay, though?"

She shook her head again, swiping at the tears that began to fall once more. "He suffered some injuries, but he recovered from them."

He wondered if Rollins was suffering the way Sera was, but didn't want to distract her by asking. His only concern at the moment was trying to fully understand what she was going through. "And driving?"

Sera met his eyes for the briefest of moments. "Is simply something I just don't want to do."

"Don't want to or can't?"

"I'm sure I can if I tried. I don't want to."

Tyler dropped his head to his chest, knowing she wouldn't admit it was a fear. Shifting sideways, he reached out, but she pushed away, planking up next to the frame of the machine. The act stabbed him in the chest, but he took no offense. She'd just told him something he was pretty certain she hadn't shared with anyone other than her therapist and maybe the other guy involved, and that meant more to him than his need to hold her at the moment. Sensing she needed some space and ready for a change of scenery himself, he took a deep breath, trying to slow the pace of his pulse, then turned the key in the ignition. The Kubota propelled forward, and they headed home.

He'd barely put the machine in park when Sera darted to the house. Trying to absorb everything she'd said and give her a few minutes of space, he waited a moment before following her in. He heard the shower running. Hoping the night didn't go downhill from here, he went to his room and pulled off his boots. Stretching out lengthwise on the bed, he closed his eyes. Being out in the sun the past two days had devoured his energy. The sunburn didn't help. His skin ached to the touch and was raw in spots, a result of the beating it took while out on the trails. His mind was just as exhausted as his body. Funny how that worked—woken from a good night's rest only to be completely drained by a small bit of information.

The incident in Afghanistan was worse than he'd imagined. His mom had made it sound like a small act, but it was much more than that. Two people had been greatly affected, one of whom suffered physical wounds. And Sera thought she was making more of her problems than acceptable. No wonder she had nightmares. Who wouldn't? Now, on top of everything else she'd endured, she was battling the fear of driving. Knowing how deeply intrusive her disorder was, he couldn't consciously walk away, leaving her to deal with it on her own. Which meant if she wouldn't come with him, then he'd have to stay there with her.

CHAPTER 17

Feeling better after washing the stress of the day away, Sera closed up the house and turned off all the lights. Certain Tyler had already gone to bed, she passed her room when she saw he wasn't there. His door was open, the light still on. He was sound asleep, though, still dressed in the dirty jeans and old ragged T-shirt from the day. She wanted to talk to him again. To better explain what happened in Afghanistan and the reasons why she didn't want to drive. She had never admitted that fear to anyone, not Rollins or her therapists, and although she hadn't meant to drop it out like she had, somehow it had rolled off her tongue easily with Tyler. Talking did help, but until now there had never been anyone that she trusted enough to do so with. Except for Rollins, but that ended up being complicated.

She wasn't sure when the two of them became more than just friends. In their first months back from Afghanistan, they spent a lot of time together. Of course that was before either realized that they were suffering any emotional effects from their incident. They talked a lot about what happened over there and then one day she recognized he was flirting with her. It was a little surprising because she'd never seen him that way, but it also excited her too. She hadn't thought of anyone romantically since Tyler and she'd missed him more than she could ever put into words since returning to the States. As badly as she hated to admit it now, the attention from Rollins was a welcome distraction from her constant thoughts of Tyler.

Unfortunately, the contentment didn't last. She noticed Rollins slowly changing. Instead of moving past their accident, he wanted to dwell on it and they started fighting when she told him she was tired of talking about it all the time. Things went downhill from there. They'd already slept together by then, which didn't help the situation any.

She felt an obligation to help him, but it was difficult when she wasn't quite sure how to help herself. He abused his medications and started drinking. When he quit coming to work, the army began the process of discharging him. Sometimes she was still angry that they'd given up on him so easily. If he'd been pushed to get help more avidly, maybe he could have worked through his turmoil, but it seemed they were all too happy to pass his troubles off to someone else. She'd tried the best she could, but he refused to listen and that was when their arguments fueled. She'd said some terrible things. Especially when it came to her feelings for him, but he hadn't held back much either. By the time he left, they were barely speaking and although he'd reached out since then, she'd refused any kind of contact back. She couldn't go there again. The constant battle of not only him, but her fears too, was more than she could handle, and she wasn't going to open herself back up to it.

Turning off the light, she rounded the bed and climbed in, not caring about the soiled clothing or layer of grime coating the hair on Tyler's arms. Not even the distinct smell of dirt and salt kept her from kissing his face and cuddling in next to him. She still had a ways to go when it came to opening up and baring her feelings like she knew she should do. Clamping down and ignoring the problems didn't help, but at least she was starting to do so without losing her temper.

Rubbing her hand along Tyler's jawline, she wondered what went through that mind of his. If circumstances had been different, who knew how the last three years would have gone? The accident in Afghanistan still would have happened and maybe her struggles would have been easier to handle with Tyler by her side; but who was to say, even if she hadn't missed that call, that they would have made it? Their relationship was tumultuous at times. Not in a physical sense, but it seemed one was always giving while the other was taking—usually her. She'd taken advantage of his love and counted on him always being there. And her actions didn't always accurately portray how deeply she felt for him. Surely at some point he would have grown tired of the act, and who knew what would have happened then? If their parting had ended more turbulently, would they have been able to forge a friendship as they had now?

Maybe the missed call wasn't a missed opportunity, but rather a chance for both of them to grow as individuals and learn how to appreciate one another the way lovers were supposed to. It might be three years too late, but she appreciated him now.

• • •

A hint of honeysuckle tempted Tyler awake. The sweet smell was like heaven to his senses. Rolling his neck to the side, he saw Sera lying closely, but with only one arm draped lightly over his shoulder.

"Hey, you," he said when he saw her eyes were open. Giving a look out the window and seeing it was dark, he asked, "What time is it?"

"Almost ten." She smiled back. "I didn't mean to wake you."

"I'm glad you did. I need a shower." Calling a truce, he grabbed the hand she'd laid over him and brought it to his lips before sitting up and pulling his shirt up over his head.

Twenty minutes later, he sat back on the edge of the bed with Sera on her knees behind him. He felt no pain from the circular pattern her fingertips made as she swirled the cooling gel around on his back. Instead of drawing out the warmth, each touch sizzled his skin more than it already did. He closed his eyes, content to sit there all night while she worked magic against his pains.

His back stiffened in an arch when her hands left, the absence of her touch a harsh reality. But then he felt a tingle in the crook of his neck, followed by a soft press of her lips against his skin. The kiss lingered in a spot that only she knew drove him mad. The kind of sensation that had him dying to wait it out, so to savor the moment, yet pushing feverously toward a powerful need for more. When her arms came around, palming the pecs of his chest, he leaned back into her, tilting his head to the side, asking for more. She gave it. Dabbing small kisses, she traced a line around the left side of his collarbone. Sparks of excitement flew south, hardening his growing bulge. The stiffness swelled as she swathed kisses around the back of his neck, giving the same attention to his left side as she had his right. He moaned when her fingers began kneading the buds of his nipples. The sound encouraged her further and he nearly came undone when her arms circled back around him, pressing the swells of her bare breasts against his back.

"Make love to me, Tyler," she murmured in his ear.

If it was possible to become intoxicated from sound, Tyler was sure he was there. Tipsy from the scent of her body wash, buzzing with heat from the feel of her hands, stoned from the beauty of her face that he could picture at any moment as if it were right in front of him. Every one of his senses was heightened. All he had to do was taste her and he'd be completely gone.

Standing, he wasted no time pulling Sera in his arms. His mouth descended on hers, taking and giving with full thrust of his tongue. Her nipples tightened between his fingers as he rolled them into round beads. She let out a low sigh when he cupped her bottom, dragging her closer, pressing his groin firmly into her middle. Another gasp came when he dipped his hands inside the hem of her cotton shorts and smoothed his hands against the fullness of each cheek.

"Baby, you drive me crazy," he whispered, shimmying her shorts down her legs. She lifted each knee, further consenting their joining as she stepped out and he tossed them aside. She was left in nothing but a pair of stripped bikini panties, and he admired the curve of her waist gliding up to the mounds of her chest. Scanning her flat stomach, he throbbed harder. Seeing a mirror of his craving reflected in her eyes, he pulled her up and instinctively she wrapped her legs around him.

Taking his time, spurring her excitement with small swipes of his tongue, he blanketed her body as he lay down. Tasting and teasing the skin along her neck, down each shoulder, to the dip in between her breasts. The mounds peaked with attention. He suckled one and then the other, licking the tinted circles, feeling Sera squirm with pleasure underneath. Every movement sent another rush of adrenaline to his groin. The lifting of her hips, welcoming his firmness against her femininity, had him aching for release. Her heavy pants begged for the same. Knowing he wouldn't last long, he encouraged her escalation. Fingering aside the thin strip of material that hindered the passage to her opening, he slid in a finger. Letting moisture collect, he treasured the wail of pleasure that bounced off her lips. "God, you're wet," he whispered, pulling out.

She panted. "Tyler."

"What, baby?"

"Please," she begged.

Sliding his finger back in, her hips lifted in satisfaction, then fell into an arch when he pulled back out. Rubbing his thumb against her most sensitive area, he pushed up in inside her again. This time, she let out a moan, while tugging at his hair. Quickening the pace, he moved against her nub until she screamed out.

As much as he always enjoyed bringing her to climax over and over before partaking in his own pleasure, it was important to him that they come together this time. Shedding his shorts and boxers, he covered himself, before peeling off her panties and throwing them aside.

His heart pounded with the race of his pulse throbbing at the tip of his head. One good thrust and he'd be done. Nudging her slick opening, he entered slowly, parting her sex with an unhurried push. She gave a low murmur of approval as he delved in deeper. Withdrawing, then pushing back in, he glided with more force the second time. The sting from her fingernails sinking into the blades of his shoulders drove him faster. Her hips thrust up with every push and pull until they found a rhythm. The pace quickened, and Sera cried out again. Then her thighs clenched, sending them both sailing over the waves of glory.

Propped up on an elbow, Tyler rubbed the back of his hand over Sera's pinked cheek. The color was evidence of the thorough grazing his unshaven jaw had made as he ravished her mouth. Their lovemaking had been fulfilling in every way.

Sera drifted off almost immediately. His body was telling him he needed to do the same, but he was afraid to take his eyes away, fearful she'd be gone if he did. He'd waited three years for her to come back to him. Had almost given up hope of it ever happening, and now that she was here, he'd do his damnedest to make sure she stayed.

She wasn't the same Sera he remembered, and at first he didn't think he'd like her new tamed-down personality, but nothing about her was repressed. She still spoke her mind. Maybe not as often or as turbulently as before, but her point was made clear. Her infectious laugh and soothing smile hadn't left and she made love to him just as feverishly as she always had. None of those things had changed. She was still the loving, caring person he'd always known. Her vulnerability was the only thing different. He didn't view it as a flaw or a sign of weakness either. In fact, the quality made her more appealing, and not in a way that made her inferior. If anything, it created an equal balance between them. She needed him just as much as he needed her.

He hadn't put much thought into the idea of her joining him on his tour. All he knew was that he wanted this to work and was willing to do whatever it took to make it happen. With his schedule, he'd be lucky to make it home a couple of days a month. A day or two here and there wasn't enough for him. For his own sanity, he needed to be with her.

But even if she had agreed, he knew now that roaming from city to city wasn't what was best. Stability in her life would be good. She hadn't really had a home to call her own since joining the army. She'd gone off to basic training in South Carolina before being stationed in Texas and then ordered to Afghanistan. Now that she was out, he figured she needed to put down her roots again. Get back into civilian life and a routine—something she couldn't do on the road.

He could already hear the string of expletives Bradley would spew when he told him he was pulling out of the tour. The guys in the band would probably be mad at first too, but once he explained his situation he was sure they'd understand. It was everyone else behind the scenes that worried him most.

CHAPTER 18

Pulling out his phone, Tyler saw Bradley's name flash across the screen. Moving his finger between the buttons to accept or reject, he tapped reject, then tossed it aside before getting up and going to the living room, where Sera was stretched out on the couch reading a book. Picking up her feet, he sat down, letting them fall into his lap.

"Get much done?" she asked, peering over the top.

"A little," he answered. "I like where it's going."

"It sounds really good."

"It did?"

"Yeah, the melody sounds fun."

The words floating through his head that morning when he'd woken were now on paper. The song still had a ways to go, but he was excited to get back to writing after taking a yearlong break. "Feels good to be writing again."

"I can't believe you stopped. You loved it as much as you did being up on stage."

Curling his hand around her thigh, he answered, "The desire just wasn't there."

"Well, I'm glad you got it back." She sat up, delivering a kiss to his cheek.

"I'm going to ride over to my dad's. Get that out of the way."

She peered at him with slanted eyes. "You sure?"

He shrugged.

Giving him a shoo away with her hand, she said, "Go. I know he's your dad and you love him. Tell him hi for me."

• • •

Sera was at the stove making dinner when Tyler came home from visiting his dad. Going straight to his room, he didn't speak, but every step he took rang through the walls. Despite her urge to run to him and see if he was okay, she ignored the discomfort and continued stirring the spaghetti sauce she'd put together.

She should have gone with him. He detested the rare visits, but she thought her and Doug's mutual dislike for one another would have only put more strain between father and son. Their relationship had been a forced one for as long as she knew. It was a relationship she thought Tyler was better off without, but that wasn't her decision to make.

Hearing him come up behind her, she turned off the stove and turned around, ready to smile, but held it back when she saw lines slanting downwards out of the corners of his freshly shaven face.

"You okay?" she asked, running her hand along his soft cheek.

"Rough day."

"I guess nothing's changed?" She wrapped both arms around his neck, and instinctively Tyler encircled her waist.

"Let's see. He was drunk when I got there. Hit me up for money and then proceeded to lecture me about why I needed to get a real man's job. Oh, and I'm pretty sure his new wife—who, by the way, looks younger than me—is knocked up. Let's hope not by him."

"I'm sorry." She dabbed another kiss along the side of his jaw.

"You have nothing to be sorry for." He returned the kiss to her lips.

"I'm sorry he's such an ass."

Tyler laughed. "You keep it real, don't you?"

"Only way to be." She smiled back then, happy that she'd livened up his face a little. "Are you hungry?"

"I am. But what do you say after we eat, we head down to Merv's for a night out?"

"I'd say it sounds like a plan."

CHAPTER 19

They stood just inside the entrance looking for a place to sit. Merv's was a favorite on Friday nights for those who drove the hour drive east into Lexington or west to the coal mines for work. It was late, so a crowd had already gathered to celebrate the end of the work week. People milled around in between tables, talking as they went while the band rang out from the stage.

Finally Tyler saw a table in the midst of being abandoned. He clasped Sera's hand tighter, tugging her in the direction of the empty seat.

He'd nearly choked when she came out of her room wearing a snug fitting pair of low-waisted jeans. Spinning around, his eyes trained in on the firm roundness of her back end. "What do you think?" she'd asked.

"I think if that top was cut any lower, you'd be changing."

The sleeveless yellow shirt perfectly accented the tan she'd gotten at the lake, but more than the ass-hugging pants or the cleavage-bearing top, the strappy black heels adorning her feet were what he favored most. She'd never been a heels kind of girl, but the look was definitely good on her and he couldn't wait to get them off when they got home.

Merv made his way over when he saw them. "Hey. Glad you two came by," he said, clearing the bottles left by the previous inhabitant into a gray tub.

"Looks like you're busy," Tyler said, looking around.

Merv let out a long breath. "You have no idea. Had a waitress get a job at the Save-A-Lot and quit on me yesterday. People talk about this town not having jobs and then when you need someone, nobody wants to work."

"Good business, though," Tyler answered back.

"That you're right about," Merv said. "Hey, you up to playing a short set tonight?"

• • •

Sera saw an old gleam sparkle in Tyler's eyes when he agreed that he would, a gleam that intensified as he walked to the stage when Merv announced to the crowd that he had a surprise for them.

A roar of whistles and clapping resonated through the bar when his name was mentioned. For a town that didn't have much, Tyler gave them something to boast about. They loved him. Yet few treated him differently. The older generation and those they'd gone to school with saw him as one of them. It was the younger kids, like the ones who'd shown up at Roy's and the few at the Dairy Freeze who he'd signed autographs for, who looked at him with envy. Somehow, Sera didn't think he went as unnoticed when he was out on the road. He hadn't said much about the attention he received, just the exhaustion of moving around, but she supposed the constant interruptions could be tiring after a while too.

She watched him walk to the stage with ease. Talking momentarily to the house band, he adjusted the microphone into position and gave the crowd a loud, "Hello, Cobb City." The bar erupted in a howl before quieting down when the beat of a drum indicated the start of a song. Then Tyler opened his mouth and belted out the first notes and in that moment she saw no worries or cares. Not even the stress from the visit with his father was there. Tyler, the rock star, was on stage. He even looked the part. Newly shaved, wearing stone-colored jeans and a white T-shirt, he exhibited his youth as he stood with a guitar slung over his shoulder. Every note, every beat, every tap of his foot, illustrated the sheer contentment pouring out of him. He loved what he did, but it was more than that. He had the ability to embed that love into one's soul and let them feel it too. Just like he'd done to her.

• • •

Sera counted up the days in her head as she lay in bed. Considering that the day was over and not counting Monday, because Tyler would be leaving early that morning, they had two more full days together. She wanted to make the best of it, but the anxiety of him leaving was starting to wear on her.

Turning to the side, she pressed her lips to his forehead. After riling the crowd at Merv's for more than an hour, they'd come home. He'd practically keeled over with exhaustion when they got into bed. She, on the other hand, couldn't make her mind quit wondering long enough for her lids to slide down. It wasn't just Tyler keeping her awake. She had a lot more floating through her head. She'd made more progress in the last three weeks than she had in over a year and she wanted to keep pushing forward. Was even contemplating buying a car and getting a job so she could keep busy when he was gone. Of course that meant she'd have to start driving, which she wasn't ready to do yet. The whole concept was frightening. What if when he left, everything went back to the way it was before? What if she hadn't made any progress at all and Tyler was merely a short vacation away from all her problems? She might fall right back into the pit of huddling in the house and thinking of Rollins day in and day out. The idea was sickening.

Concerned for what his departure might bring, she was even considering his request to join him on tour. The offer seemed ideal, except she'd be dependent on him in so many ways. The financial aspects didn't bother her so much. She had money saved that would get her through. It was her emotional instability that had her concerned. Being unable to drive was the biggest issue. She couldn't expect him to be at her disposal twenty-four/seven. He was a busy man and busy men didn't need needy girlfriends tagging along. That alone made her point for the second problem. She didn't want to need Tyler. She wanted to be his equal, because that was the only way to keep their relationship fair without the struggle of taking and giving.

Sitting up on the edge of the bed, she reached for her first sleeping pill in days.

• • •

Tyler woke with a shift in the mattress. Seeing Sera on the edge of the bed, he asked, "You all right?"

"Yeah. I can't sleep."

"Something wrong?"

"No. Just one of those nights."

"Come here." He reached out, pulling her back into his arms. "Want to talk about it?"

"I'm restless, is all."

Running his hand through her hair, he said, "Then why don't you talk me back to sleep?"

"Am I that boring?" She scoffed, lifting her head from his chest and throwing him a teasing smile.

"Baby, anything but. Your voice is soothing, though."

"I think I want to buy a car."

The quick shift in conversation had him spinning. Buying a car seemed pointless if she wasn't going to drive it. Unless she was trying to tell him she was ready to give it a go again.

"Did you hear me?" she asked.

"I did. It seems kind of silly, though, to buy a car when you're not driving."

"I'm going to ask Merv for a job. I'll need a car to get back and forth to work. So, I guess I'll have to start working on the driving issue."

"I'm not comfortable with you working at Merv's."

"I've got to do something, Tyler. I can't sit around here every day."

"Then come with me."

The talk with Bradley hadn't gone well that morning. Actually it had gone worse than he'd imagined. Bradley was very honest in his thoughts. He believed canceling the tour was a career-ending move and that Tyler would be throwing away his talent, not to mention damaging his reputation. He was still waiting to hear back from all the other people who had a hand in putting his tour together—most importantly, his label, but it didn't sound good. Maybe if he could talk Sera into coming, they could somehow make it work for now, and then in February they could start concentrating on putting down roots.

"Don't start on that again," she said.

"I'm not starting anything, I'm simply telling you how I feel."

"And I feel I'm not ready."

"Fine," he relented, in no mood to argue. "We'll go look at cars, then."

CHAPTER 20

Tyler stood with his heart pounding in his ear. Knuckles white, the paper in his hand shook as he reread the last sentence. *I don't understand how you can love someone who nearly killed you.*

He'd come home from a trip to the grocery store not finding Sera anywhere in the house. He did find her bedroom door open and mail strewn across the bed. The return addresses were all the same: Lucas Rollins of Welch, West Virginia. Picking up a picture tucked underneath one of the envelopes, he stared at a camouflage-clad man smiling widely at the camera. There was nothing but sand in the background. Turning it over, he saw the name Rollins written in Sera's handwriting on the back. His hand shook. The picture wobbled up and down. Then, giving it a fling, it fell to the bed.

Turning his attention back to the letter in his hand, he saw his name and read on. *Do you think Tyler loves you? He chose his career over you. He left you when you needed him. I was there. I was there for you, not him.* His jaw tightened. The son-of-a-bitch was making presumptions he knew nothing about. Teeth gritted, he glanced back down at the pile of letters, seeing another picture. Pulling it out, he saw Sera's arm locked around Rollins. Both were dressed in their desert uniforms, both smiling just as profoundly. His gut rolled.

"Hey, I didn't hear you come back."

Tyler's head snapped up at the sound of Sera's voice. His eyes met hers, just as she realized what he held.

"What are you doing?" she snapped, snatching the letter and picture from his hand.

He had no explanation. It was wrong to intrude on her privacy, but he hadn't been able to help himself when he saw the opened letter sitting there. "He was in love with you?"

Sera stuffed the single sheet of paper back into the empty envelope. Her eyes shifted from the letters laid out to the cardboard box sitting next to her bed.

"He didn't love me," she said. Bending over, she began stacking the letters into a pile.

"He said he loved you, Sera." His eyes filled with hatred for a man he didn't know.

"Apparently you didn't get to the one where he called me an ungrateful bitch."

She gathered the mail, shuffling it in her hand.

"He said I almost killed you."

"He said a lot of things." She blew the accusation off.

"Dammit! This isn't funny."

"No, it's not," she barked back. "I walk out on the back porch to take a call from Uncle Roy and I come back to you snooping through my things."

"I wasn't snooping."

"Then what do you call it?"

Looking away, he felt shame, yet didn't regret what he'd done. "I was curious."

"Well, then, you know what? Be curious all you want." She slung the letters to the floor. A heap puddled at his feet. The door frame rattled as she turned and left.

•••

Sera didn't know exactly how much time passed before her bedroom door opened. Long enough for Tyler to read all of what Rollins had written and then some. Enough time for her to gather her wits and be ready to explain any questions Tyler might have. She didn't so much care that he'd read them. She hated that he'd picked up that one in particular, but any of the others didn't bother her, because once he got through them, he would see

Rollins didn't like her, much less love her. What made her mad was that he'd taken a piece of something and assumed he knew all about the relationship she and Rollins had. What they'd had was so complex she didn't understand it most of the time.

Hearing the back door slam, she got up to see where Tyler had gone. He was at the tree line before she spotted him. His leveled shoulders and brisk stride told her everything she needed to know. He wasn't curious. He was mad. Scary, angry mad.

"Tyler," she yelled, bounding down the steps. The drizzle from the threatening showers hit her arm. "Tyler," she yelled louder as he disappeared into the woods. Taking off in a jog, she slipped on the damp grass and tumbled in a low hole. "Shit," she muttered, getting up. The pressure she put down on her foot caused a slight limp. "Tyler!"

Passing the line of trees outlining the outer edges of her uncle's property, her eyes scanned the thicket for movement. The ground sloped upward from there. Her ankle throbbed with tenderness every step she took. Paying little attention, her ears strained to hear. Nothing came. "Tyler, please," she begged.

Taking a rest, she sat down on the ground, twisting her ankle to loosen it up. It would likely be sore the rest of the day, but it wasn't sprained. "I don't know what you're upset about." She wasn't sure where Tyler was or if he could hear, but she talked anyway. "I wish you would talk to me, though."

"Like you talk to me?"

She glanced to the right where the voice had come from. The dark brown shirt he'd put on that morning blended perfectly with the poplar tree he was slumped against. Getting up, she covered the twenty steps between them, then knelt down on both knees. "What's wrong?"

He stared off in the distance. The dampened shirt clung to his thick chest, and trickles of rain beaded at the tips of his hair.

"You probably think I deserve your silence, and maybe I do. But I can't fix this if I don't know what's wrong," she said.

"So he was the guy?" Tyler asked with bitterness.

Determined to be forthcoming and honest, so not to make this worse, she answered. "Yes."

"I read every one of them. Some of them twice."

"I left them there for you to read."

"No, you threw them at my feet, mad because I invaded your privacy."

She sat back on her heels. "I was throwing them away. I wasn't reminiscing like you think. I just … I wanted to read through them one more time before I burned them."

"God, I hope you weren't reminiscing about the day I almost killed you."

"You didn't almost kill me."

"He thinks so." He wedged his legs up between his stomach and arms, forcing a barrier between them. "Shit, Sera. You were thinking of me when it happened."

Moisture pooled in the corner of her eyes. "I never wanted you to know that."

"He knew it."

"I felt guilty for not being more aware and for what happened. I felt I owed him an explanation."

"So what he wrote was true? The train whistle you thought you heard made you think back to the night I asked you to marry me?"

She swallowed hard. "Yes."

"Fuck." Tyler kicked out his legs. "I don't know what I'm more pissed about. The fact that I'm responsible for all you've gone through, the fact you had feelings for this guy, or the shit he wrote about you."

"You're not responsible. It happened, Tyler. Even if I had been focused like I was supposed to be, nothing would have changed that. And he's hurting. He can't help the way he feels."

Tyler laughed dryly. "So you can stay guilt ridden over it, but I can't?"

"I hold myself accountable for what happened when we got back, not for what happened over there."

"He loved you."

Meeting his gaze, she shook her head. "No, he didn't. He cared for me. We latched on to each other because we shared a common tragedy, but we didn't love each other." Needing some kind of harmony, she reached out to touch his knee. "I accepted that. He didn't."

"So you didn't love him?"

"In the way I love Maggie? Yes. But like I love you? No."

The hard edge around Tyler's mouth softened. "You love me?"

He asked as if he didn't know the answer, but his soft smile gave him away. He'd always known she loved him, even when she doubted it herself. Reassured that they were going to be okay, she climbed into his lap, pushing her fingers through his hair. "I have always loved you."

He cushioned his head against her breast. "I've always loved you too."

CHAPTER 21

Despite Tyler's encouragement for her to keep them, Sera threw every one of the letters away. He thought she was trying to make him happy, when really it was her way of letting go of the past and the guilt Rollins had over her head. The letters were painful and erratic. One minute, he professed his love and the next he hated her because she didn't love him back. He accused her of being heartless and emotionally unavailable. He even described her lack of desire for intimacy as a personal flaw. Some of what he said was true. She hadn't been able to invest her heart in their relationship, because her heart still belonged to Tyler and it was hard for her to be intimate with him when she knew they had no future together. She read the letters so often, she had most of them memorized and each time she did so, the guilt festered more, keeping it a permanent part of her. Moving on meant she had to let go. That was what Dr. Khazi had said anyway, and that was what she was trying to do.

It seemed their spat that morning was all but forgotten by the time they finished dinner—at least on Tyler's behalf. Not that Sera let it interfere with enjoying the rest of the day, but every time she looked at Tyler, she wondered what he really thought or if he blamed himself like he said. With only a day left, she didn't want to fiddle around and presume anything. And she wasn't going to pretend it didn't happen to avoid another argument. She was done with that.

Resting against the door of the living room, she watched Tyler scribble words in the notebook he'd been using to write his song. His brows furrowed when he flipped the pencil over to erase something, then his eyes widened as he reread the corrected version. Happy with the result, he tucked the pencil between his teeth and thumbed his guitar.

Hating to interrupt the beauty of his sheer concentration she cleared her throat, saying, "Want to go for a walk?"

Looking up, he cocked his head to the side with slanted eyes. "Is this a 'we need to talk' walk?"

"It's an 'I need some exercise and yeah, we need to talk' walk." She smiled, hoping to give him the confidence that she didn't want this talk to turn into a fight.

He nodded, sighing heavily. "Okay."

• • •

Tyler intertwined his fingers with Sera's as they headed across the yard. The silence between them threatened the resolve he'd come to about canceling the tour. The no-news-is-good-news theory wasn't sitting well. No news meant the tour hadn't been canceled yet. He was supposed to return to Nashville the day after tomorrow and wasn't sure what he would do if he hadn't heard anything from Bradley by then, and now Sera wanted to talk. He was pretty sure she hadn't changed her mind about going. Once she made a decision about something that was usually how it went. So what she could possibly have to say now he didn't know, but he hoped like hell it wasn't more bad news, because he wasn't sure how much more he could take.

They turned left at the mailbox; instinctively he knew they were headed to the train tracks. He abhorred the idea. He still saw it as a terrible coping mechanism, but Sera insisted it was a part of the healing process. He wondered if she'd ever be the same. The problem with trains was easily understandable, but he'd noticed other things too. She'd flinched when a gun went off on the TV the other night, and a couple of times when the screen door banged closed, he could see the startle in her eyes. She rarely looked at the road when they were driving. Instead her head would drop down to her lap or she'd stare out the passenger window.

She downplayed her condition. Maybe she wasn't as emotionally battered as some of the other soldiers coming back from war, but it didn't mean she didn't need help. He wanted to be that help.

"So, what do you want to talk about?" he asked when they were halfway there.

Sera angled her head to the side. "We're not going to fight. Okay?"

"Is that a promise?" He squeezed her hand.

She nudged him back with her shoulder. "You're the one who developed a temper. Maybe you should be the one promising."

"For the record, it's completely unfair that I have to talk when you're ready to do so, but you get to run off and avoid me."

"Hey. I've been better."

"Yes, you have." He threw an arm around her shoulder, kissing the top of her head. "So what's on your mind?"

"I don't want you to blame yourself, Tyler."

"It's kind of hard not to."

"Listen to me." She stopped, turning toward him. "You didn't pay attention to what I said happened."

Crinkling his eyes, he said, "I think I paid damn good attention."

"The area was deserted. Subconsciously or not, I chose to ignore it. Rollins and I were talking. I was already distracted. I didn't start thinking about you until I thought I heard the train whistle. By then it was already too late."

Trying to digest that, he grabbed her hand and started walking again. "Did you ever blame me?"

"No," she answered with a shake of her head.

"Never?"

"You were what I thought about when I realized my life might end. How could I blame you?"

He stopped walking when her voice cracked. "Babe, don't cry." Smoothing her hair back away from her face, he dried the tears with his thumb, then bent in and kissed her. "It makes me happy to know you were thinking about me."

"Every day." She sniffled.

"Yet you were mad as hell when you saw me," he teased, taking her hand again.

"I said I didn't blame you for the accident. I didn't say I forgave you for breaking my heart. Leaving a voicemail was brutal."

"We've been over that. You know I'm sorry."

"I know." The teasing curve was back in her lips. "But that doesn't mean I can't give you a hard time about it."

"All right, I was an ass."

"Yes, you were, but I didn't make it easy on you."

"Let's not go over this again."

"We're not. But there's something I want you to know."

"What?"

"I never believed you'd cheat on me." Sera leaned her head over onto his shoulder. "I'm sorry. That was a horrible thing to constantly accuse you of."

Tyler pulled her head closer, kissing the side of her face again. "Thank you. I needed to hear that."

Seeing they'd made it to the tracks, Sera turned them back toward Roy's.

"Now that we both agree what a jerk I was, can I ask you something?" he asked, taking the opportunity to get more answers to some questions he still had.

Sera kicked at a rock. "What do you want to know?"

"How bad are the nightmares?"

"They aren't really nightmares. They say it's anxiety. I have trouble falling asleep because my mind won't quit obsessing over what happened."

"So it's not like they portray on TV where you wake up in the middle of the night, pouring sweat, thinking you're back over there?"

"I'm sure some cases are. I've had a few bad dreams, but they're sporadic."

"But trains …"

"Always trigger the memories. Anything that sounds like a train or train whistle makes me think about it."

"Do you think that will ever go away?"

"Probably not."

"That sucks."

She laughed. "Yes, it does, but my old therapist explained it to me like this: It's like listening to a love song and it reminding you of a recent breakup. You're always going to think of that person when you hear the song, but the more you hear it and the more time that passes, the easier the pain gets."

"It makes sense when you put it that way. Can I ask what you obsess about? Is it the incident itself, or …"

Kicking another rock, she answered, "Mostly him and what he became."

Tyler loosened his grip on her hand and hung his head toward the ground. Disliking someone he didn't know wasn't something he made a habit of doing, yet every time he thought of the man who Sera had shared so much with, he felt a burning in his gut.

"We're not fighting, remember?" Sera reiterated, strengthening their grip.

"I'm trying not to hate him, but it's hard after reading everything he wrote about you and knowing the two of you were together."

"That's really unfair since you slept with other people too."

"I didn't have feelings for any of them, though."

• • •

Not seeing lack of feelings as a defense, Sera didn't want to fight either. "He was a friend. That's all. And you shouldn't hate him. He's the product of a terrible situation. It could easily be me in his shoes. In fact …" She paused. "I was headed there." She left out the part that Tyler had been a saving grace to her, in a sense. If their reunion hadn't come when it did, who knew the shape she'd have been in by the time Roy came home from Florida? Being alone and struggling wasn't a good combination.

"So what happened exactly?"

"Are you asking about us sleeping together or—?"

Laughing, Tyler said, "No, please spare me the details." Then, shooting her a jab with his elbow, he said, "I'm talking about the rift between the two of you."

She had been joking about explaining their sexual relationship, but sleeping together was part of the rift. Not knowing where to begin or how to protect Tyler's insecurities, she started from the beginning.

"We knew each other before Afghanistan, but for one reason or another we became closer when we got over there. Going through what we did together strengthened that bond." She thought back to their first weeks back in the States and the time they spent talking about what happened. She'd told Rollins everything, including her feelings for Tyler.

"It helped having someone who understood what I was feeling, but after a while the constant rehashing kept the pain fresh and I knew it wasn't helping. I tried making him understand that but by then he'd already started declining. Drinking, abusing his meds, and he missed work a lot. I watched him sink deeper and deeper, knowing he was pulling me with him and I needed to get away, but I was committed to helping him."

"So how did you get away?"

"He was discharged."

"Like you?"

"Yep, except his was quicker because of his emotional instability."

Tyler raised an eyebrow, questioning her further.

"I flat out refused to do my job."

"Driving?"

"How'd you guess?" She tossed him a grin, happy that they were able to talk about this so sensibly. It was so different than any of the other weighty talks they'd had weeks or even years before. "I'm just thankful they gave me an honorable discharge."

"When was the last time you heard from him?"

She thought. "The last letter came about ten months ago. I never responded to any of them, so I guess he gave up. As far as I know, he doesn't even know I'm out."

• • •

Tyler remembered all the things he'd read earlier in the day. The first few notes were short with the guy saying he missed Sera and hoped she was doing fine. A few apologized for the way he'd acted before leaving the army. It was the ones that professed his love that Tyler started noticing his hostility. He wanted to punch the guy in the face for the names he'd called her. Yet, oddly enough, he also felt bad for him too. He knew what it was like to feel as if you'd lost everything and how easily it was to sink into a hole—because that was what it felt like when he lost Sera. Compared to what Rollins had endured, though, his problems were small, so he could only imagine the pain the man was going through. Anyone with a conscience would feel for him. Whether he'd hurt Sera or not, they'd shared something that Tyler couldn't understand, and he could at least appreciate that she'd had Rollins to confide in when he wasn't there for her.

CHAPTER 22

Tyler threw his phone down on the bed. The call back from Bradley went much like he'd predicted. The label wasn't happy about the tour being postponed. He was an up-and-coming artist. Promotion of the record was essential. Bradley relayed the message most likely just as it had been told to him. He'd been so brash as to let Tyler know he wasn't anyone who would be missed if he fell off the radar for a few months.

Bradley was right. Tyler didn't have enough hits under his belt to make a difference to the public. There might be a few diehard fans who followed his career, but if he took a break now, his chances of reclaiming his current status would be difficult. When you were at the top, you had to keep going; otherwise you fell away into no man's land.

It didn't help that Bradley reminded him of his place on the shit list from the release of "Box of Regrets," and that further damage to the relationship with his record label may happen if he didn't quit pushing their buttons. Again, Tyler knew everything Bradley said was correct, but he asked him to plead his case again anyway.

Running his hand through his hair, he thought about what to do. Sera didn't know about his decision. Knowing how she'd react, he kept putting it off, hoping Bradley would give him something positive to offer when he did tell her. Like, *Sure, canceling a headlining tour that embarks in four days is no problem.* Instead, it was more like, *Hey, honey, I'm about to be broke, unemployed, and possibly sued for breach of contract, but at least we have each other.* He'd be okay with that. Wouldn't he? They'd make it. There were plenty of jobs and he could get his music fix playing weekends at Merv's.

Who was he kidding? He loved being on Merv's stage again, but in no way did it compare to the satisfaction he felt playing larger venues. He'd be content, but the craving for more would always be there.

•••

Sera poked her head in Tyler's room, asking if he was ready to go. Looking at cars wasn't the way she wanted to spend their last day together, but anything to keep busy was a better alternative to wallowing in the worry of what his absence in the morning would bring.

"Yeah." Tyler nodded. "Just give me a minute."

Suddenly Tyler looked as tired as he did weeks ago. Lines marked his face. The newly bronze color of his skin had taken on an ashy haze. "Are you okay?" she asked.

"Yeah."

"If you don't feel like going we don't have to."

He stood, tucking in his shirt. "I'm all right."

He didn't look all right, though. His posture was stiff, his jaw set, and there wasn't an ounce of warmth radiating from his eyes. Thinking that maybe he was just as anxious about what the morning would bring, she decided not to push. "Okay, I'll be in the living room when you're ready."

His mood didn't change during the drive to Lexington. In fact, he grew even more dire the more time passed. She tried bringing him into conversation about the tour, hoping the topic would rile him up and get him excited about the event, but he deflected the subject each time. Halfway there, she was ready to turn around and go back home. The prickly air had her thinking that finding a car when she still refused to drive did seem silly. It wasn't like she could take it home if she found one she liked, but today wasn't about buying a car. It was a step forward, a step she wanted to take, and she wanted Tyler there for it. But when Johnny Cash rang out for the third time since they left the house, Tyler turned his phone face down on the seat. She knew the icy manner was a result of him having other places he wanted or needed to be.

• • •

Tyler stopped at the first Ford dealership he saw. Meeting Sera on the passenger side, he glanced over the lot and pointed to a row of midsize cars. "Those over there look good. Why don't you start? I'll catch up with you. I need to make a call real quick."

"Sure."

He waited for her to walk away, then hit Bradley's number. He'd called three times in the span of an hour. It was either really good news or very bad.

He held the phone to his ear. Bradley never said hello when he answered.

"There's no option to postpone. If you pull out, you're done."

Leaning back against the truck for support, Tyler rubbed at his temples, trying to ease the sudden pounding in his head.

"Did you tell them that I had some personal things going on?"

"They don't care. They said they have too much money tied up in this already. We're at the last damn minute, Tyler. What did you expect?"

He had no words. He didn't know what he expected.

Bradley continued. "Rob Marshall himself said your ass had better be back in Nashville on Tuesday for the radio interview with WTEN."

So it had already gone straight up to the president of the company. His stomach knotted further. "And if I'm not?"

"Tyler, don't push this. You're a liability to them at this point. Tickets are sold, merchandise is on its way. Salaries have been paid. That's not even considering all the other things that went into making this tour happen. It takes a lot of money to pull something of this caliber off."

He exhaled sharply. "I know."

"You got the real deal here, man. A headlining tour. Do you know how long it takes most artists to get that?"

He did—years, sometimes more than a decade. Nashville had only been his home for almost four years. "I do."

"I don't think you do. You're willing to walk away from it."

"I'm not asking to postpone indefinitely. I just need a couple of months." Sera was getting better every day. In two months, he was sure she'd be out tearing up the roads of Cobb City in her new car. If not, maybe by then he'd be able to at least convince her to come with him.

"They've already said no. It's now or never."

"Never as in what, exactly?"

"As in your contract will be canceled. Rob hadn't spoken with anyone in the legal department to know if they would file breach of contract yet. Like me, this was thrown at him quickly."

Again, Tyler was lost for words as the comprehension of what his decision might cost sank in. His head now felt like it was going to explode.

"Think about the fans you'll lose," Bradley continued. "What's it going to be like to go back to playing some two-bit honky-tonk as you try to work your way back up to the top again? Trust me. Once you fall it's hard to get back up. Tyler, think about this. Think about it hard. This is your career you're playing with."

He had done nothing but think about it all day. He didn't see any other option, though. "I can't do it. I'm sorry."

Bradley sighed. "You're putting me in a lousy position here. As your manager, it's my job to tell you when you're making poor decisions and right now you're making a terrible mistake. Not only for yourself, but for the band and myself. Have you considered how selfish this is? You aren't just screwing this up for you. The guys are a part of Tyler Creech. They're going to go down with you. Not to mention how poorly this will reflect on me. I'm not at all happy about my reputation being tarnished just because you don't want to leave your girlfriend."

Tyler ground his teeth together. Sera's situation was more than that, but Bradley was doing a fine job of making him feel guilty.

"I don't get this, Tyler. We've worked hard to get here and now you're tossing it away. You're not the only one who's busted his ass the last few years. We all have."

Tyler swallowed back more guilt. His lack of response allowed Bradley to continue.

"You need to get your head on straight and quit dicking around. You have until the morning to figure this out. I'm supposed to call Rob back by then and I'm sure if I don't have good news, he'll have an answer from their attorney." With that, the line went dead.

Pressing his hands to his temple in an attempt to combat the throbbing, Tyler took in a deep breath. The choice he'd made a few days ago seemed easy. Now, knowing either way he went he could possibly lose something he loved, it didn't seem fair.

CHAPTER 23

Sera was standing next to an older aged salesman when Tyler found her. The glare she shot him revealed her annoyance. He didn't want to add her to the list of problems he had, but it seemed inevitable with the way the day was going. Trying to deflect both of their moods back to what they had come for, he asked, "Find anything?"

"I think she's interested in this little blue thing here." The salesman flashed Tyler a mouth full of white and pointed to Ford Focus behind them.

"I thought you were looking at those SUVs over there?" He threw his head in the direction he'd first sent her.

"No," she said sharply. "You wanted me to look at those."

Sensing her temper, he put aside his uncertainties for the safety of the small car, willing to appease her for the moment. "I thought you'd want something a little bigger. This is nice too." He bent down, peering in the window. Walking around to the backside, he gave it a once-over.

"Want to take it for a test drive?" the eager salesman suggested.

"No," Sera spit out.

"Let us look inside," Tyler said, before opening the driver side door. The new car scent smacked his nostrils. "Looks nice." Stepping back, he waved his hand for Sera to get in. "See what you think."

"That's all right." She shook her head.

Rubbing her upper arm, he whispered, "You don't have to drive. Just sit in it. See what it feels like."

He held his breath as she stepped forward, then unsteadily climbed in. Concentrating on the way her cheeks crumpled with unease, he cursed when a vibration had him pulling his phone out of his pocket. Seeing it was Mark, his lead guitarist, he held up a finger to Sera indicating he'd only be a minute. Already answering as he turned his back, he told Mark it wasn't a good time and that he'd call him back. Turning back around, he bent down to eye level with Sera.

"You okay?"

She shook her head, breathing in deep. Her hands wound tightly around the steering wheel, the anxiety of her condition plastered all across her face. He was proud of her. Simply sitting inside was a huge accomplishment, yet he didn't want to make a big deal and bring attention to her fears. He was looking at the radio on the console when his phone buzzed again. He ignored it, letting the music play to voicemail.

Glancing over into the backseat, he commented, "I like it." Another buzz; the caller was persistent. "Do you want me to take it for a drive?" The buzzing came again.

"Aren't you going to get that?" she asked with disdain.

If he didn't, it would just keep ringing. "I'm sorry. Give me a few more minutes."

"Hey," Tyler answered, moving a couple of cars over, so he could have some privacy.

"What the hell's going on in Redneckville?"

His friend and drummer Jayson took every available opportunity to rile him about his upbringing. Tyler called him a city slicker every chance he got. "Man, you don't even want to know."

"Yeah, I think I do. Brad called. Said you were pulling out on us. Please don't tell me this has something to do with a woman."

Tyler cringed as he admitted, "It's Sera."

"Oh … oh! Sera. You mean army chick Sera?"

"Yeah. She's out of the army, though."

"So what's going on? You two getting back together or what?"

"Something like that," he answered. Although they hadn't specifically addressed what they were doing, he had no doubt he and Sera had a future together. That was, if he could get through the day without royally pissing her off.

"What's the problem, then? Bring her along."

"It's not that easy. She's got some things going on right now."

"Man, I don't know what to tell you. I get that you love her and have for a long time. But now is not the time to let a woman drive you crazy."

His head dropped. His lungs heaved in a deep breath. *Too late for that. She'd been doing it for years.*

"Ty, listen. You know whatever you decide I'll have your back, but this is a pretty big deal. Mark's called and so has Levi. They aren't happy about this. I have to say, I'm not crazy about it either. It's kind of messed up. This was our big break. Not to mention the money we'll lose. What could be so important that you'd throw all of that away?

Tyler closed his eyes when he said, "She has PTSD." Even now, he hated the thought of it.

• • •

Stretching her hands out until the tingling sensation stopped, Sera resumed her hold on the steering wheel. The hard plastic curled underneath her fingers was both terrifying and exciting at the same time. The thrill of being in the driver seat wasn't something she'd expected. It was her own stubbornness that kept her from driving. Not a fear or threat that she might do something wrong. She could drive. She knew that. It was like a bicycle. Once you learned, the foundation never left. Her worry was that, like the train, every time she was behind the wheel she might float back to that sun-filled day. She would do anything to keep that day from taking over her head—anything.

Her heart pattered a little dance. The urge to cry was prominent, but it was tears of joy. She wasn't thinking about Afghanistan. She was happy, except not so much with Tyler. His mood and his lack of interest in the progress she'd just made irritated the hell out of her.

Giving the car another look, she got out and thanked the salesman for his time, informing him she was interested, just not today. Then, taking in a small circle of the lot, she saw Tyler positioned between two cars. His wide shoulders snapped back tight and high as he raked a hand through his hair repeatedly. What he was suddenly so stressed about, she didn't know. The idea of it being solely about leaving didn't seem right with all the calls of the day, though.

She smoothed her hands against her jeans and took in a deep breath, exhaling slowly. He was headlining a major tour in three days and she was sulking because he wasn't paying attention to her. *Nice, Sera.*

Tyler didn't say much on the way home. Then again, it was hard to have a conversation when his phone rang every few minutes. He never took the calls. He either rejected them or he let it ring until his voicemail picked up. After about the eighth or ninth time, he turned the phone off completely. Seeing his obvious distress, Sera wished the people who dictated his life would leave him alone so that they could enjoy their last evening together. But between the silence and constant interruptions it didn't seem possible.

By the time they were almost home, she needed to find an end to the discomfort, afraid if she didn't, the day would finish out just like the afternoon had gone: quiet and unsettling. She couldn't go through the next few hours like that. She needed some kind of reassurance that they'd be all right once he left, so she asked him to stop when they came to the railroad crossing.

Tyler darted a rough glare. "Not tonight. I can't do this tonight."

She wasn't sure what he meant. All she wanted was to talk, but then, realizing where they were, that he probably thought she wanted to wait for a train. "I just want to talk."

"We can talk at home."

The forceful way *talk at home* came out was a loud and clear message that he had something to say too and that she likely didn't want to hear what it was.

Craziness filled her head with all sorts of ideas drumming up. Was she just a fling? Did he ever have intentions for them to have a future together? If not, then what was all the talk about her going with him? Her hands began to shake, her stomach churned, and her pulse flew away. Once more, she was completely confused and questioned her judgment. Something hadn't been right all day. She'd wanted to believe it was, though, and had written it off as a part of the hectic life Tyler led.

Pressure built behind her lids. The dam was ready to burst. She wanted to let it go, to bury her hands in her face and bawl her eyes out, but he'd seen enough of her tears the last three weeks. She wasn't giving him the privilege of seeing any more.

CHAPTER 24

Tyler pulled to a stop in front of Roy's. Turning off the engine, neither he nor Sera got out. His distance that day had drawn a wedge between them again and as unintentional as it was, he couldn't help it. Between the calls from his band and another one from Bradley, his nerves were fried. Jayson, although not happy about it, understood. No one else did. The abundance of text messages he'd received in response to his ignored calls let him know how they felt. The only thing they understood was that he was stomping out their biggest break as a group and he'd made the decision without consulting them first. He realized how unfair it was now. The band might carry his name, but there were five other men who contributed. As it stood, his recording contract wasn't the only thing he might lose. If he didn't board the bus on Wednesday, he might very well lose some damn good musicians too.

The longer they sat there, the thicker the air became. The pressure was unbearable. Inhaling deeply, Tyler tried to forge some relief, then rolled down the window to let in some fresh air. Looking out, he finally said, "I canceled the tour."

Sera spun around. "You what?"

"I canceled the tour. I'm staying here."

Fumbling with her seatbelt, she threw it over her shoulder. "Why on earth would you do that?"

He propped an arm up on the door. "Because you need me."

Her temper flamed just like he knew it would. "I need you?" The sarcasm poured out of her mouth. "You're walking away from your biggest break because I need you? Well, that's just stupid."

He winced. "I don't see it that way."

"I don't need you, Tyler!"

Pulling on the handle, she gave the door a shove with her shoulder and jumped out. She was at the steps before he could catch up.

"I can't consciously leave you like this," he confessed.

"Maybe your conscience should have spoken up when you kept calling me out for not being open with you," she shouted back. "When did you decide this, anyway?"

His head hung. The decision he'd made without consulting others who were involved was coming back to bite him. "A few days ago."

"Ha." She laughed sourly. "Well, did it ever occur to you that maybe you should have told me about it before now? Jesus, you're supposed to leave in the morning."

"I was waiting to see what my record label had to say."

"And what did they say?"

"It doesn't matter."

"The hell it doesn't. You've worked too hard for this. I'm not letting you screw it up. What did they say?"

He hated to say the words. "They'll void my contract."

"Void. What does that mean, exactly?"

"It means I lose the deal I currently have." He was signed on for one more record, but recording another album was the least of his worries. He left out that he could be sued for breach of contract. He hoped it didn't come to that.

• • •

Her feet heavy with every lift, Sera ascended the porch stairs slowly. Her hands hadn't stopped shaking since Tyler told her they needed to talk. She fumbled with the zipper on her purse. Snagging it, she had to close it up to get it back on track before trying again.

The talk wasn't anything like she'd imagined. Instead of dumping her, he told her he was staying. That should have made her ecstatic, but the fact that he was doing so because she needed him shot anger straight through her heart. She'd been clear about not wanting his pity and all along that was exactly what he'd been doing.

Opening the door with a shove of her shoulder, the weight of the tears gave way. Streams rolled over her cheeks. She didn't bother to wipe them away. Her wounded pride was the least of her worries.

Dropping her purse inside the door, she pummeled down the hall to Tyler's room. Closing and locking the door behind her, she sank to the floor. Sobs, deep within, sneaked to the surface. She jammed her fist to her eyes, trying to absorb the wetness. It didn't help—as soon as she moved them away, the moisture collected again.

And to think she'd been starting to feel whole again. She'd begun eating more and sleeping better. She was able to maintain focus and keep on task. She laughed. She smiled. And she'd cried—something she rarely let herself do. The tears hadn't stopped falling since Tyler arrived. She'd felt all the things she'd been keeping buried inside. It was coming back to her. She was coming back. Unfortunately, Tyler didn't see that. All he saw were her wounds and she was afraid that was all he was ever going to see.

Standing with purpose, she grabbed the suitcase sitting on the floor by the closet and tossed it onto the bed. Then, picking up the pile of clean clothes that sat on top of the dresser, she started packing his suitcase.

• • •

Tyler jostled the doorknob. "Sera, open the door."

No answer. He knocked, then tried to open it.

"Sera, open the damn door."

Nothing came. Giving the door a whack with the palm of his hand, he tried again. "Sera, open the door and talk to me."

After several more minutes of pleading and pounding, he gave up. Sliding down the wall to the floor, he sat, trying to figure out a way to make this right. The repeated stress of the day caught up with him. His whole body, inside and out, ached as if his zest for life was drained. There was no reason to keep wasting what little energy he had left trying to get Sera to open the door and talk to him. She was being unreasonable again. No matter what he said, he wouldn't be able to rationalize his decision with her now. Time and space were her only friends at times like this. When she calmed down, she'd be easier to talk to. Unfortunately, time was of the essence. "Can you at least tell me what you're doing in there?"

She didn't answer right away. He thought for sure she'd continue to ignore him. A few minutes passed.

"Packing," she finally said, so low he barely heard. "I won't let you do this."

"Don't you think I should have a say in what I do?"

"Did you think to consider my thoughts when you decided that I needed you to stay here and babysit me?"

Hearing her more clearly, he knew she was just on the other side of the door. So close, yet so far away. "I've been doing nothing but thinking about what was best for you since I saw you standing out in the yard. The fact that we are having this conversation shows that."

"This isn't what's best for me. Jesus, Tyler! I carry enough guilt. I don't need you adding to it."

He stood, leaning sideways against the door. If he could just get her to open up. "You have nothing to feel guilty about. It's my choice."

"You're making that choice because of me."

She was there. Two inches of wood was all that divided them. He wanted to reach out and touch her. No, he needed to. He needed her. "I did it for me." He waited for a response. When nothing came, he continued. "I didn't do it because you need me. I did it because I need you."

Forever seemed to pass. The drawn-out silence had Tyler wondering what Sera might be thinking or if she'd listened to anything he'd said. Finally he heard the click of the lock. He stepped back as the door eased open.

She stood, her arms wrapped around her stomach, on the other side of the threshold. The streaks of red painting her cheeks burned his gut. Stepping in, he scooped her to him, planting his face in the crook of her neck. He breathed her in, holding her close, never wanting to lose the feeling of having her in his arms.

"You need to go," she whispered, tears streaming again.

He firmed his hold around her waist. "I need to be here."

"No," she declared.

"Then come with me," he asked, his voice breaking. "Maybe I'm a selfish bastard for asking, but come with me. Please."

Stepping back, she wouldn't look at him. "I can't. If you don't leave, I will."

He called her bluff. "Where will you go?"

"My mom's."

His eyes cast to the floor before looking back up. Sincerity reflected back at him. She would find a way to Chicago tonight if he stayed and that was the last place he wanted her. He was pretty certain Sylvia couldn't provide the support Sera needed. Closing his eyes, he turned to the side. His throat balled tightly. Nodding forward, he said "Tomorrow. I'll leave tomorrow."

"Tonight," she answered, handing over his suitcase. "Tomorrow will only make this harder. I need you to leave tonight."

CHAPTER 25

It wasn't Tyler's beautiful lashes puddled with moisture Sera kept thinking about. Nor the hurt she felt when his eyes went askew every time she looked at him. The way his mouth twisted in a knot as he gathered the rest of his things stabbed at her heart, but she could push that aside too. It was the picture of the back of his head, as he walked out the door, that she couldn't rid her mind of.

The haircut he'd needed three weeks ago was now long overdue. The dark strands had lost the curl to their ends, but still hung in a thick wave. It was the only wave she got. He didn't kiss her goodbye or so much as bid a farewell hug. He stood in the doorway for a moment, letting her take in all his hurt and confusion, before saying, "Don't do this. Fight for us, Sera." She nearly did. Her mind said go, but her feet stayed planted, and when she had no response, he shut the door and left.

He called twice, breaking her heart further each time the phone rang. The first call came roughly two hours after he left. The other she assumed was when he arrived back in Nashville. Both voicemails asked that she please talk to him. She was tempted, very tempted. She wanted to hear his voice more than anything and not through a recording. She wanted to know that he was going to be okay, but doing so would accomplish nothing at this point. He would ask her to come again and she'd refuse. Then they'd argue their points until it turned into a yelling match—or worse, a repeat of three years ago.

There were two text messages when she woke. Again, he asked her to call and again, she chose not to. They both needed space to put their lives into perspective and remember what was important—his career and her recovery. Keeping hope that if they both kept that in mind, they might still have a future together, she made herself get out of bed and face the day. She forced down a bowl of cereal, barely tasting her favorite brand. A shower gave her some energy, but she lost the will to do much after that and ended up on the couch the biggest part of the day. Taking turns staring at the ceiling and doodling on a pad of paper, she cried off and on for hours, until she was sure she couldn't cry anymore.

He didn't call that night, but he sent another text late.

Busy day tomorrow. Radio Interview with WTEN in the morn. Meetings afterwards. Leaving in 2 days. We need to talk. I love you.

Each time he reached out, she lost some of the willpower to keep distant. She missed the low, soothing sounds of his voice that lulled her to sleep and his high-pitched cackle that made her laugh. She grieved for memory of the way his eyes crinkled together when he was being sarcastic or funny, and how her skin tingled from his touch. Her body ached from the loss of being surrounded in his arms. The knotting and cramping of her stomach kept her from eating anything further after breakfast, any hunger blinded by the sorrow. The tightness in her shoulders exuded up into her head. The haze from little sleep and perpetual tears left her in a fog. She hadn't felt this disturbed since returning from overseas and she wasn't sure that she'd been this physically distraught then. Rollins hadn't crossed her mind in days, and all her worries of slipping back into the austerity of his memory seemed for naught now. The only thing fueling her misery was not being with Tyler.

CHAPTER 26

The six o'clock alarm was a cruel awakening after battling another night's sleep. More bouts of crying kept her up late into the night and when she couldn't drift off even after the tears dried up, she reread Tyler's last text and spent the next thirty minutes Googling the radio station he'd mentioned.

Now, at precisely seven thirty, she sat balled up in the corner of the couch waiting for the eight o'clock morning show to start. She'd already downloaded an app to her phone so she could hear the interview. Her ears perked every time a song came to an end, thinking he would be there. Five minutes after eight, she started worrying that maybe there was another WTEN in some nearby city other than Nashville and when the host announced yet another song, she dropped her phone into her lap. Unable to sit there through the torment, she was just about to get up, when he chimed back in. "*Up next, Tyler Creech is in the studio to tell us what it was like meeting George Strait for the first time.*" Her heart skipped into a fast rhythm as her hands clutched her phone snugly to her ear.

It was a sweet kind of torture when she heard the host welcome him on air. The seconds ticked by until his deep raspy sound echoed through the room. She hung on every word, internalizing everything from the pitch of his voice to the answers he gave. He was barely on air five minutes—long enough to discuss the record, his recent hit, and how much he enjoyed what he did, before they took a break. It seemed like the commercials went on forever before they came back on and Tyler told his story of meeting George Strait while in the bathroom at the recording studio. Another break followed, tantalizing her already frazzled nerves. Then the interview wrapped up with news of the tour before the first notes of her heartbreak began to play when "Box of Regrets" was introduced over the radio.

Eyes flooding, she buried her head into the arm of the couch. She had hoped to hear enthusiasm for the journey he was about to embark on. She wanted proof that what she had done was right. But all she heard was the same stressed-out Tyler who had shown up at Roy's three weeks ago and left two days before.

They were both losing. He was miserable. She was miserable and for what reason? *What's wrong with things being easy?* He'd asked her that the second night out by the train tracks. And hadn't she promised herself that if she ever found happiness again she'd embrace if fully? So what if she needed him? He needed her too.

Knowing he was busy, she beat the temptation to reach out immediately and instead tried to keep busy while she waited for his call. The day was long. No amount of laundry or cleaning took her mind off of him. He was there and always would be.

By nine that night, she'd almost given up, but then her phone rang.

Tingling with anticipation, she answered. "Hey."

The hope quickly dispelled when he answered back, "Hey."

The ragged texture of his voice was alarming. Call it intuition, but she knew something was definitely wrong and it wasn't just the strain between them. "Is everything okay?"

"I'm fine, but …"

That was all she needed to hear for the worry to start. Anything Tyler might have said directly afterwards was rebounding off her eardrums. A pain stabbed down her neck through her shoulder stirring up the unsettled nausea. Doubling over, she sat down at the kitchen table, trying to make sense of what he was saying. She opened her mouth to ask, but the burning in her throat forced her to clamp it closed.

"But what?" she finally let out, then stopped when the heaves of her chest captured her breath.

"I'm okay. It was just a little accident."

"What kind of accident?" she expelled with a whimper.

"A deer ran out in front of me and I swerved, rolling into a ditch. My truck isn't nearly as lucky as the deer."

"But you're okay?"

"Yeah. It's just a broken foot and a good-sized bump on my head. They're keeping me overnight just to make sure."

"Where?"

There was hesitation in his voice when he said, "Lake Cumberland Regional."

Gaining some ground on the shock of learning he was back in Kentucky, she stood, already on the move. Pulling out the junk drawer next to the refrigerator, she fumbled through it looking for the spare set of keys Roy told her was there.

"Sera, I'm sorry …"

"Stop!" she blubbered through falling tears. She did not want to talk to him. What she had to say couldn't be done over the phone. She had to see him for herself, so she knew he was all right. Tucking the keys down into her pocket, she shot through the kitchen and living room, grabbing her purse on the table by the door. "I can't talk to you about this right now."

CHAPTER 27

Taking a deep breath, Sera sat behind the wheel of her uncle's Toyota Corolla. She hadn't driven in more than two years, had tried once when her commanding officer demanded that she follow an order to do so. Her refusal had earned her a trip to get a psych eval, and that was the beginning to the end of her time in the military.

Since then, it was her stubbornness that stood in the way. No one, not even the army, was going to make her drive until she was ready—except Tyler. She was so mad at him now that the initial shock had worn off. Aside from the roughness in his voice, he sounded fine. And he had called, therefore he was capable of moving around, so he couldn't have been terribly injured. But she wouldn't be okay until she saw for herself.

She sat idling the car for a few moments, waiting for the right moment to let go of all the past. As soon as she turned the key, she knew it was gone. All the fears, all the guilt, she had nothing left to hold her back. That had been the biggest problem all along: fearing that if she moved on, somehow she was betraying Rollins who hadn't been able to do that. Tyler was right; there wasn't any reason life couldn't be simple. Pulling down the gear, she let her foot off the break and felt the car roll forward. Someday, she hoped Rollins would be able to understand that too.

The first hour of the drive should have only taken forty-five minutes. Cars blew past her on the highway. A few even honked their horns when she wouldn't speed up. Someone in a Subaru flipped her the bird as they sped out around into the adjacent lane. If her hands hadn't been knuckle-clutching the wheel, she would have returned the gesture. She didn't care. There was a slow lane for a reason and she wasn't doing much under the speed limit anyway.

She did better the second half of the drive when the main interstate turned into a two-lane highway. She thought a lot about both Rollins and Tyler in that last thirty minutes. Two men who were both carved deeply in her heart, but only one of them she loved. At least loved in a way she didn't want to live without. How unfair she'd been to use her condition as an excuse to deny a love that was once in a lifetime. Well, in their case, twice in a lifetime and she sure as hell wasn't going to push her luck with a third.

Sliding the car to a stop between two white lines, she killed the ignition and threw the keys in her purse, making sure to hit the lock button before she dashed inside. She didn't slow down until forced to wait on the elevator. After hitting the up button twice, she turned around, ready to take the steps to the third floor. A ding and parting of the doors had her turning back around. Stepping on, she was thankful it was empty as she tried to rein in her breaths.

Every door she passed, she looked at the number, knowing full well Room 325 was still several doors down the brightly lit hallway. Pausing before coming to the end, she combed a hand through her tangled hair, embarrassed for the way she looked, and heard several voices bellowing from inside the door on the right. Confirming it was the right room, she stepped in.

Her eyes immediately surveyed the man lying in the bed. Making sure all limbs were intact, her gaze traveled down the patterned gown, catching on the large blue air cast swaddled around his right foot, then back up to the gauze taped to his forehead.

"Hey," she said when Tyler saw her standing there.

"Hey," he answered back with a beaming smile.

There were two other men in the room. A man wearing a baseball cap and jeans sat in the corner, while one dressed in a suit stood at the head of the bed. She gave them each a nod hello before taking a spot next to Tyler.

"Sera, this is my manager, Bradley." Tyler pointed to the man standing on the opposite side of her. "And that's Jayson, my drummer, over there in the corner."

Both men said their own hellos. She smiled back appropriately, suddenly feeling like an outsider.

"I didn't think he'd pull something like this just to get out of the tour," his manager said, interrupting the awkward moment.

Tyler grinned. Sera didn't return the sentiment. Her eyes grew wide with suspicion. Surely Bradley was joking. Tyler wouldn't have gone to these lengths just so he could cancel the tour. Before she could ask though, Jayson stood, saying he was headed out, with Bradley following behind.

When the two men were gone, she sat down on the edge of the bed, clasping her hand around Tyler's. "Please tell me he was joking."

He chuckled. "Yes, sweetheart, he was joking."

"Then what are you doing back in Kentucky?"

Slow to answer, he said, "Coming back for you."

"Even though I told you I wasn't ready?"

"You wouldn't take my calls or return my texts. What was I supposed to do?"

"You were supposed to get on that tour bus in the morning and live your dreams."

"I was. But I'm fighting for you this time. I wanted us to live our dreams together."

Feeling the tug of emotion already, she wrapped both hands around his. Her eyelids tighten despite her attempt to stay calm. A tear spilled over, and she wiped her face against the sleeve of her shoulder. "I'm not going to win here, am I?"

"Probably not," he answered back, a glimmer of hope seeping out of his eyes.

Standing, she dried her face and climbed up in the bed. Hospital rules or not, she wanted him to hold her. Resting her head on his shoulder, he wrapped his arms around her.

"And exactly what was your plan when you got here?" she asked into his chest.

"I had twelve hours before the bus left. It's a five-hour drive each way, therefore I had roughly an hour or so to convince you to come with me. Other than that, I didn't have a plan."

"Cutting it close there, cowboy." She laughed.

"I don't want to do this without you, Sera. It has nothing to do with you needing me. I'm the one who needs you. We can make this work."

"I know," she replied. "I listened to the interview this morning. You're not happy and neither am I—I'm miserable. And I do need you. We need each other."

He kissed the top of her head. "So you'll come?"

She nodded. "Will they postpone the tour?"

"For a few weeks, until I can get around without crutches."

"I have to get Roy's car back home, though."

"Why didn't y'all bring Maggie's car?"

"Maggie's not with me."

"Who brought you, then?"

She swallowed back more tears. "I drove." She bit down on the inside of her bottom lip as her eyes flooded. Not out of sadness, but with relief and pride of how far she'd come.

He hugged her tighter. "Baby, I'm proud of you."

Needing some space to catch her breath, she sat up, corralling the river on her face with her wrist. "It's crazy what you'll do when you really want something."

Rubbing a hand over her thigh, he winked. "Kind of like throwing your career away for someone you love?"

"Yeah, something like that," she answered, smiling back. "By the way, how's the truck?"

He rolled his eyes. "The truck isn't totaled, but it's going to be a while before she's back into shape."

"Maybe you just need to get a more sensible truck."

"Hey, I like my truck."

"I don't think I'm going to like driving it, though." She wrinkled her nose.

"You'll just have to get your own sensible mode of transportation, then."

"What about a bicycle?"

"Honey, I don't think a bicycle is going to be all that sensible for your trips back home to visit Roy."

Laughing, she said, "Probably not."

"That reminds me." Tyler eased up in the bed. "Open that drawer." He pointed to the table beside his bed. "Jayson had to rescue it out of the truck for me, but there's something in there for you."

Opening the drawer, she was a little nervous about what she might find, then recognized the small, square cardboard box and her own handwriting addressing it to Tyler. A lump lodged in her throat as she picked it up. "You kept it." She swallowed, the flow of tears starting again.

"Of course I kept it."

Taking out the smaller velvet box, she opened the lid and looked down with eyes wide at the tiny engagement ring Tyler had bought for her when he was only nineteen.

"I lied, Sera. I did have a box of regrets. This was it. The day I got this back in the mail was the day I knew I'd regret losing you for the rest of my life."

She could barely see through the moisture as Tyler slid the ring back in place where it belonged and would never leave again.

"I have every intention of getting you something bigger, but I hope this one will do for now." Looking nervous, he asked, "Marry me, Sera. I'm asking again … will you marry me?"

"Tyler." She kissed his lips. "I don't need a bigger ring. All I need is you."

EPILOGUE

Sera quit fiddling with her hands as soon as the car came to a stop. Even with the bit of excitement that came with what the day might bring, she couldn't make herself look up and instead stared down at her lap. Her nerves did somersaults inside her belly, making her rethink the sausage and biscuit she'd eaten early that morning. She'd passed on lunch when they stopped an hour ago. Eating wasn't an option until she got this over with.

Unaware of the breath stuck at the back of her throat, she let it go when she felt a hand cover the top of her thigh.

"Hey," Tyler whispered. "You all right?"

Blowing out a puff of air, she took in another deep gulp and finally looked up to see his handsome face marked with a crinkle of worry across his brows. She was happy that he was driving again now that the cast was permanently gone. Although with the schedule they'd kept, there hadn't been time for anything fun while out on the road. Like he'd said, the days were exhausting, yet satisfying too. He loved what he did and she loved being there sharing the experience with him. Being together at least cured the loneliness. Besides, she knew it wouldn't always be like this. Tyler had promised to slow down. They planned to take time off this spring so that she could finally get settled into their Nashville home.

"I'm nervous," she said, clasping her hands together.

Tyler reached up, smoothing back her hair behind her ear. "He sounded good on the phone."

Eyes falling back to her lap. "You should have told me what you were up to."

Tilting her head up to look up at him, Tyler answered. "You're right. I have should have and I'm sorry."

Blinking back the tears trying to form, she knew her apprehension was misplaced. She wasn't upset with Tyler. The fact that he'd gone to the trouble of tracking down Rollins and even set aside time so they could meet up with him only proved further how much he really loved her. Her worry came from not knowing what she was about to see. Rollins had told Tyler his life was going well, but that could have been a ruse. She hadn't known about this meeting until last night after Tyler's show in Charleston when he told her they weren't moving on with the rest of the gang. She hadn't even thought about how close they were to Welch, West Virginia, when they crossed the state line a day ago. Tyler had, though, and he'd been planning this for weeks.

"I'm just afraid he's going to be just like I remember," she uttered.

"But what if he's not?"

Rolling her eyes, she grinned. "You always look at things so positively."

"Someone's got to," he teased.

Entwining their fingers together, she looked him in the eye. "Thank you."

"For what?"

"For being the husband I always knew you would be."

They'd flown to Florida four days after Tyler was released from the hospital and were married on the beach with no one but Roy and Diana present. Now, two months later, she hadn't regretted the decision for a moment. Leaning over, she kissed him on the cheek. Trying to ease her own tension, she said, "Not many men would hunt down a guy their wife slept with to set up a meeting between the two."

"Darlin', I'm not most men." No, he wasn't. "Besides, I told you that doesn't matter. The only thing that's important to me is that you're all right. And you're not. You still feel guilty about him."

"I can't help but feel that way. I feel like I let him down. We were friends and I turned my back on him."

"Be his friend now. I'm pretty sure that's him sitting right over there."

She followed Tyler's finger pointing out the window to a bench in front of the coffee shop where they were meeting Rollins. It was him. Wearing jeans and a large brown coat, his uncovered blond hair was still trimmed short in a military-style cut. He wasn't smiling, but wasn't frowning either and for a moment she wondered how he felt about seeing her. That was until she noticed he wasn't alone. A woman bundled with a heavier dark blue coat and matching scarf sat holding his hand. Her brightly colored copper hair peeked out of the hat she wore. Even with the layer of clothing Sera could see her belly protruded out in front.

Pulling her coat around her middle, Sera stepped out of the car. The late November wind smacked against her face, making her thankful for the warmth Tyler's arm gave as he wrapped it loosely around the small of her back. Putting on a smile, they made their way toward Rollins and his friend, but her smile faded as soon as Rollins's eyes flared with recognition and he stood with open arms. Embracing the hug he offered, she buried her head into his chest. Trying to hold back the tears streaming down her face, she failed miserably. After several attempts, she gave up and let them fall. For several long minutes, they stood enfolded together before Rollins finally pulled back. Even through the cluster of emotions strewn across his face, she saw a glimmer of the buoyant man he'd been when they'd first met.

"It is good to see you," he said, before holding out his hand to shake Tyler's. "Luke Rollins."

"Tyler Creech," Tyler said, returning the handshake thoroughly.

"And this is my wife, Leslie." Rollins pulled the very pregnant woman to his side.

Sera said hello as she dried the remaining tears, then followed behind the couple as they went inside the coffee shop. She was a little nervous when Tyler and Leslie took another table to give her and Rollins privacy to catch up. She liked having Tyler there, but also knew that she and Rollins wouldn't talk about the things they needed to with others around.

The first few minutes were spent trying to get over the awkwardness of seeing one another. *How have you been? Fine. How about you? Good.* Rollins told her he worked for the highway department and that his and Leslie's baby was due in February. Sera listened, happy that Rollins really did seem to have it together.

"I can't believe you didn't tell me Tyler Creech was the Tyler you were engaged to."

Rollins angled his head toward the table where Tyler and Leslie sat. A handful of people gathered, wanting pictures and autographs. Used to the interruptions, Sera turned back to Rollins, feeling guilty for never sharing that bit of information with him. He knew she was engaged when they met, but at the time, Tyler was still struggling to get his name known, so it hadn't seemed important, and the two of them were over by the time she and Rollins grew close.

"It wasn't a big deal," she played it off.

"Wasn't a big deal? You married him. That's a pretty big deal."

"I did," Sera threw back, smiling. "What can I say? He drives me crazy." Then, putting it in terms that only Rollins would understand, she said, "Actually, let me rephrase that. He drove me sane."

That was exactly what Tyler had done. He'd taken her mangled soul and driven her not back to the person she used to be, but to a better version of the woman she once was.

"It's good to see you happy, Sera."

"You too," she answered back.

That was all that needed to be said. Happiness was all either one of them had ever wanted for the other.

About the Author

Dena grew up in central Texas, but has lived in the foothills of Kentucky with her husband and two sons long enough to call it home.

She loves writing stories of happily ever after, as well as taking road trips with her family. She has an affinity for all kinds of music, but is partial to her southern roots.

You can see what she's up to at *www.demiro1029.wordpress.com*, on Facebook at *www.facebook.com/denarogerswrites*, or on Twitter @Demiro1029.

A Sneak Peek from Crimson Romance
(From *Heart of Design* by Ellen Butler)

"Sophia Hartland, put that tray down and come with me right now!" Poppy hopped from one foot to another, her face agitated.

"But Hannah said they need more shrimp." I tried to carry the heavy-laden tray past her.

"Oh, bother Hannah!" Poppy grabbed the tray out of my hands and shoved it into the hands of a passing waiter, hired for the night. "Pedro, take these out to the main buffet table and replace the empty."

The surprised Pedro nodded and headed back out into the throng of party guests.

"Here, put some of this on." Poppy handed me a tube of lip gloss from her pocket. She reached behind my head, and, undoing the alligator clip, allowed the heavy, dark tresses to fall down my back. She ruffled the locks with her fingers.

"What are you doing?" I stood with an opened tube of gloss in my right hand and tried ineffectually to grab with my left the clip Poppy had removed from my hair and attached to her pants. "I need that! It gets too hot with my hair down."

She grabbed me by the shoulders, and, with a hearty shake, got my full attention. "Sophie! Ian O'Connor wants to meet you!" Her hazel-green eyes bore into me.

"Okay. Who's Ian O'Connor and why does he want to meet me?"

"What! Are you kidding? Do you live in a hole? Ian O'Connor! You know, Eeeaann Oh-Coonnneerr." She said it like I was deaf and could read her lips if she spoke nice and slow.

I shook my head, completely lost.

"He's one of the hunks on the hottest new cop show this year, *LA Heat*. It was a mid-season replacement in the spring, and it's been picked up for a full season this fall. He's so smokin' hot, women throw their bras at him. You know, he plays Ryder McKay."

"Nope." I shook my head. "Sorry. Not one of the shows I watch. Why does he want to meet me?"

"He said he liked the painting in the front hall and asked who did it. I was pseudo-stalking him, and thus in hearing distance, so I cozied up and explained all the credit went to you, my best friend and interior designer," Poppy said in a rush. "And he said he'd like to meet you sometime. And I said, 'well she's here tonight' and if he was serious I could introduce you two." She bounced up and down like a rabbit and squealed, "And he said, 'sure.'"

I rolled my eyes, always the cynic. "Poppy, he probably happened to mention it in passing, and then when you attacked, he was just being nice. This guy has likely made a beeline to another part of the house by now to get away from you, crazy stalker woman. We'll be lucky if he didn't already bolt from the party."

I loved Poppy dearly. She was my best friend in LA, and as the owner of Poppy's Party Planning, she gave me jobs that helped supplement my income when times were slow, and I was between design contracts. I met my intelligent, crimson-haired friend at a party six years ago, early in her career. This job was for a director's birthday party, and Poppy had come up with the idea of going old Hollywood and asked for my help with the party décor. I decided nothing screamed old Hollywood like art deco and created an entire theme around it. Unfortunately, Poppy had a quirky tendency to fall in and out of love with TV and movie actors as often as she changed her socks. I feared Ian O'Connor was her latest fixation.

"Please tell me we aren't doing 2 a.m. drive-bys with this Ian fellow."

"Sophie!" she exclaimed. "You have it all wrong. Ian's not my latest crush. Seriously, he wants to meet you. Do you have one of your business cards?"

I always carried business cards with me, especially to Poppy's Hollywood parties. I hoped to break into the A-listers and dreamed of becoming the "it" designer. So far, my business saw mild success, but I had yet to work on a big director's or actor's home.

Pulling a card out of my pocket, I fluttered it in front of her face. "Okay, stalker lady, if this guy is still around, take me to him."

"Here. Use this on your nose. It's shiny." Poppy handed me a small compact and to please her, I powdered my straight nose, wiped a black glob of mascara from beneath my blue-eyed lashes, and slicked on strawberry-flavored lip gloss. My dark hair was ruffled, giving me a slight bedhead look.

"Have you got a comb? My hair is a mess."

"It looks good. You know, sexy messy, like one of those Victoria's Secret models."

I rolled my eyes again. I was about as far from a Victoria's Secret model as you could get. My wavy hair fell just above my bra line when it was down, which was rarely. I was about five seven and currently wore a size eight, which was thin for me. However, in LA, a size eight was pretty much comparable to a rhinoceros when a majority of the women prancing around wore a size two. Poppy, her patience finally at an end, snapped the compact shut, grabbed my hand, and dragged me into the party mob to search for the elusive Ian.

Ian apparently wasn't that elusive; Poppy ran him to the ground at the bar. All I could see was a head of dark, wavy hair and an incredible set of broad shoulders. His back was to us, and he was engaged in a conversation with a sylph-like creature barely wearing a white dress.

I jerked back from Poppy's grasping hand. "I don't think now is a good time. He's busy talking with someone. Maybe I'll meet him later tonight."

"C'mon. Don't be a chicken. Mr. O'Connor. Ian, yoohoo." Poppy waved a hand, her bracelets jingling merrily.

Ian turned and caught Poppy's eye. She crooked her black polished finger, and, much to my surprise, he disengaged himself from the sylph and strolled our way.

Taking a gander at Ian from the front was even better than seeing him from the back. He was one of the many "beautiful people" inhabiting the LA-Hollywood scene. I couldn't see the color of his eyes in the gloom, but the face was well worth looking at. A chiseled jaw and strong cheekbones flexed as he took a drink from the dark beer bottle and licked his lips. He clearly worked out on a regular basis, because his pectorals were perfectly formed and part of a tattoo peeked out from beneath the tight blue T-shirt, which clung to a rock-hard bicep. The air pressure surrounding me dropped, and my mouth went arid as his six-foot-plus frame approached.

"Ian O'Connor, meet my good friend Sophia Hartland, designer extraordinaire."

I blushed at Poppy's intro and subtly wiped a sweaty hand on my pants before taking his warm, caressing grip.

"It's lovely to meet you, designer extraordinaire." He spoke with a slight Irish brogue. He held my hand a moment longer than necessary.

Oh, lord, it wasn't enough that the looks made my heart speed up; the accent was going to put me over the edge. I could see why Poppy was crushing on this dude. I cleared my throat. "You, too, Mr. O'Connor. Poppy's a big fan of your show. She was telling me all about it."

"What about Sophia Hartland? Do you watch my show?" He flashed a perfect, white, toothy Hollywood grin.

I shook my head. "No, I don't care for cop shows."

That got a rumbly laugh. "Ouch. You're the quite the foil to an actor's ego."

Oh, geez. I grimaced. Twenty seconds with this guy and I'd insulted him. I was completely thrown off my game and saying whatever popped into my head. Generally, I had more tact. I knew better at these swanky parties. I needed to be all smiles and ingratiating to get more clients. Unfortunately, toad-eating didn't come naturally to me.

"Sorry. What network is it on? I'll set my DVR to record it. I'm sure I'll love it." I glanced around for Poppy to save me from myself.

She must have wandered off or been called away. Suddenly, I was in a crowded room one on one with this handsome Irish thespian, making an utter fool of myself.

"No, no. Don't apologize. Your first answer was best." His chuckling died down.

"Umm … listen, Poppy said you liked the art deco theme I put together. So … um … here's my card." I thrust the little piece of cardstock at him. Yikes, this was so unusual for me. I never lost my cool over a guy, especially an actor. I mean come on, an actor? What was it was about this dude that was making me behave like a stuttering idiot?

"That'd be grand. I just moved into a new place and figure it needs a lady's touch, so I could have a fancy party like this." His Irish accent pulled out the a's and rolled around in a singsong lilt.

I was relieved to be on a topic where I couldn't fail. "Sure. I'd love to see your place and work with you to create a luxurious space that makes you feel comfortable and yet is great for entertaining. If you want to give me a call, we can set up an initial consultation. I can see your home, and we can determine your style."

He smirked. "Not sure I've got a style, luv."

Back on my A-game, I put on my ingratiating business smile. "Oh, everyone has a style. Sometimes it just needs to be developed and refined. Maybe you're right, and a lady's touch is just what you need." I lightly tapped his solid forearm.

A very tall, very thin Barbie doll blonde with long, flat-ironed hair, wearing a strapless red dress and five-inch heels minced up and cooed at us. "Ian, honey, a group of us are gathering in the billiard room to play pool. Come play with us." She pouted. The way she hung on Ian's arm shouted possessive girlfriend, and the glare she sent my way declared, "hands off."

"Who's this?" Barbie simpered.

"Tanqueray, this is Sophia."

Tanqueray? Really? I did a mental head slap.

Tanqueray thrust an empty champagne glass into my hand. "Sophia, why don't you be a sweetheart and get me a refill. Can you bring it to the billiard room?"

"Hold up, Tanqueray. Sophia's an interior designer. She's not the waitress."

Barbie doll eyed my black pants, sturdy black shoes, and tailored white button-down, which clearly identified me as one of the wait staff. Her eyebrow rose in disdain.

I stuck on a honeyed smile. "Actually, I am working tonight. I help Poppy when she's short on staff." I laid the champagne glass on a passing waiter's tray and shifted my gaze back to Tanqueray, speaking directly to her with my faux smile.

"Tanqueray, Tommy the bartender is right behind you," I pointed over her shoulder. "*He* can get you whatever you need."

She made a tsking sound as her jaw dropped. Dismissing her, my eyes locked back to Ian. A muscle twitched at the corner of his mouth, and an eyebrow rose. *Oh crap.* I couldn't tell if he was irritated or amused by my dismissal of his girlfriend. I decided I'd better try to make nice and get the hell out of his presence before producing any further *faux pas*.

"Mr. O'Connor, why don't I put together a tray from the buffet and have it sent to the billiard room? It was nice meeting you." With that, I turned on my heel and strode out of sight.

Ten minutes later Poppy found me in the kitchen banging my head against the pantry door.

"Hey, Soph, what's wrong? Why are you abusing the pantry?"

"I royally screwed that up. This could have been my big chance to get into the Hollywood crowd."

"Uh-oh. What happened?"

"I allowed Ian's girlfriend to get under my skin and I was rude to her, right in front of him. I don't think he was impressed." Clunk, clunk went my head.

"Okay, honey. Stop that. You're going to leave a bruise on your forehead." She pulled me away. "C'mon. It couldn't have been that bad."

I explained our conversation.

"Ugh. Tanqueray? Seriously?" Poppy peered at me.

"Seriously."

"Gee whiz, I would've given Ian more credit than to date a woman named Tanqueray. I mean really, who the hell names their kid after a bottle of gin?" Her throaty laugh lightened my mood.

"It's probably a stage name. She looks like a slasher." Slasher is the title Poppy and I'd given to the hundreds of wannabe model slash actresses who crawled the streets of LA like cockroaches.

"Don't beat yourself up over it. There are other Hollywood schmoozers here. Why don't you take half an hour to do some networking? I'm sure you'll score a new client."

So, I handed out five more cards. Two were to Hollywood spouses, one to the wife of a producer and the other to a director. The rest ended up in the clutches of trophy girlfriends, what Poppy and I called hangers-on, also known as "entourage" to bigwigs, the people actually making the money. I didn't hold high hopes of obtaining an actual client out of anyone except possibly one of the trophy girls.

Poppy sent me home around two in the morning when the party had wound down to about two dozen older guests. All the young starlets and actors gathered their entourages around midnight and moved onto the latest "it" club to see and be seen. The maneuverings of the Hollywood grind made me glad I wasn't trying to become a slasher. There was too much relying on looks, weight, and whether or not you were liked by certain producers and directors. I was content to have my business, good friends, and my dog. Anything else was overrated. Or at least that's what I liked to tell myself.

In the mood for more Crimson Romance?
Check out *An Inconvenient Love* by Alexia Adams at
CrimsonRomance.com.